D1135326

It was a force of nature, Jess's smile. Ben felt it down deep in his gut. His flesh leapt.

This is not *what I need right now.*

But then he thought...*why not?* He'd finished with his latest in a long string of socialites. What was to stop him from exploring this attraction further?

Ben almost laughed. Because this wasn't just attraction he was suddenly feeling. This was lust—an emotion he was not unfamiliar with. But this time it felt stronger. Much stronger.

Impossible to ignore.

Impossible not to pursue.

He could hardly contain the burst of triumph he experienced when she noticed him assessing her, and he heard her sharply indrawn breath, watched her reef her eyes back to the road as if the hounds of hell were after her.

And perhaps they were, he thought darkly. Be damned with his conscience! Be damned with common sense! He had to have her. And soon.

Miranda Lee is Australian, and lives near Sydney. Born and raised in the bush, she was boarding-school-educated, and briefly pursued a career in classical music before moving to Sydney and embracing the world of computers. Happily married, with three daughters, she began writing when family commitments kept her at home. She likes to create stories that are believable, modern, fast-paced and sexy. Her interests include meaty sagas, doing word puzzles, gambling and going to the movies.

Recent titles by the same author:

MASTER OF HER VIRTUE
CONTRACT WITH CONSEQUENCES
THE MAN EVERY WOMAN WANTS
NOT A MARRYING MAN

TAKEN OVER BY THE BILLIONAIRE

BY
MIRANDA LEE

First published in Great Britain 2014
by Mills & Boon, an imprint of Harlequin (UK) Limited,
Eton House, 18-24 Paradise Road, Richmond, Surrey, TW9 1SR

© 2014 Miranda Lee

ISBN: 978-0-263-24340-6

Harlequin (UK) Limited's policy is to use papers that are natural,
renewable and recyclable products and made from wood grown in
sustainable forests. The logging and manufacturing processes conform
to the legal environmental regulations of the country of origin.

Printed and bound in Great Britain
by CPI Antony Rowe, Chippenham, Wiltshire

TAKEN OVER BY
THE BILLIONAIRE

CHAPTER ONE

MURPHY'S LAW STATED that if anything could possibly go wrong, then eventually it would.

Jess did not subscribe to this theory, despite the fact that her surname was Murphy. But her father was a firm believer. Whenever anything annoying or frustrating happened, such as a flat tyre when he was driving a bride to her wedding—Joe owned a hire-car business—then he blamed it on Murphy's Law: bad weather at the weekends; down-turns in the stock market. Recently, he'd even blamed the defeat of his favourite football team in the grand final on Murphy's Law.

Admittedly, her dad was somewhat superstitious by nature.

Unlike her father, Jess's view of unfortunate events was way more rational. Things happened, not because a perverse twist of fate was just waiting to spoil things for you without rhyme or reason, but because of something someone had done or not done. Flat tyres and stock-market crashes didn't just happen. There was always a logical reason.

Jess didn't blame Murphy's Law for her boyfriend suddenly having decided last month that he no longer wanted to drive around Australia with her, having opted instead to go backpacking around the whole, stupid world for the next year! With a mate of his, would you believe? Never mind that she'd just gone into hock to buy a brand-new four-wheel drive for their romantic road trip together. Or that she'd started thinking he might be Mr Right. The truth, once she'd calmed down long enough to face it, was that Colin had caught the travel bug and obviously wasn't ready to settle down just yet. He still loved her—he claimed—and had asked her to wait for him.

Naturally, she'd told him what he could do with that idea!

Neither had Jess blamed Murphy's Law for recently having lost her much-loved part-time job at a local fashion boutique. She knew exactly why she'd been let go. Some cash-rich American company had bought up the Fab Fashions chain for a bargain price—Fab Fashions was in financial difficulties—and had then sent over some bigwig who had threatened the managers of all the stores that, if they didn't show a profit by the end of the year, all the retail outlets would be closed down in favour of online shopping. Hence the trimming of staff.

Actually, Helen hadn't wanted to let her go. Jess was an excellent salesgirl. But it was either her or Lily, who was a single mother who really needed her job, whereas Jess didn't. Jess had a full-time job during the week working at Murphy's Hire Car. She'd only taken the weekend job at Fab Fashions because she was mad about fashion and wanted to learn as much as she could about the industry, with a plan one day to open her own boutique or online store. So of course, under the circumstances, she couldn't let Helen fire poor Lily.

But she'd seethed for days over the greed of this American company. Not to mention the stupidity. Why hadn't this idiot they'd sent over found out why Fab Fashions wasn't making a profit? *She* could have told him. But, no, that would have taken some intelligence. And time!

Before she'd been let go last weekend, she'd asked Helen if she knew the name of this idiot, and she'd been told he was a Mr De Silva. Mr Benjamin De Silva. Some searching on the Internet just this morning had revealed a news item outlining the takeover of several Australian companies—including Fab Fashions—by De Silva & Associates, a private equity firm based in New York. When she looked up De Silva & Associates, Jess discovered that the major partner and CEO was Morgan De Silva, who was sixty-five years old and had been on the Forbes rich list for yonks. Which meant he was a billionaire. He was divorced—surprise, surprise!—with one son, Benjamin De Silva: the idiot they'd sent out. A clear case of nepotism at work, given his lack of intelligence and lateral thinking.

The office phone rang and Jess snatched it up.

'Murphy's Hire Car,' she said, trying not to let her irritation show through in her voice.

'Hi, there. I have a problem which I sure hope you can help me with.'

The voice was male, with an American accent.

Jess did her best to put aside any bias she was currently feeling towards American males.

'I'll do my best, sir,' she said as politely as she could manage.

'I need to hire a car and driver for three full days, starting first thing tomorrow morning.'

Jess's eyebrows lifted. They didn't often have people wanting to hire one of their cars and drivers for that length of time. Mostly, Murphy's Hire Car did special events which began and ended on the one day: weddings; graduations; anniversary dates; trips to Sydney airport; that sort of thing. Based on the central coast a couple of hours north of Sydney, they weren't an overly large concern. They only had seven hire cars which included three white limousines for weddings and other flash events, two white Mercedes sedans for less flash events and one black limousine with tinted windows for people with plenty of money who wanted privacy.

Recently her father had bought a vintage blue convertible Cadillac but it wouldn't be ready for hiring till next week, having needed new leather seats. Jess knew without even looking up this weekend's bookings on the computer that she wouldn't be able to help the American. They had several weddings on. Not uncommon given that it was spring. 'I'm sorry, sir, but we're fully booked this weekend. You'll have to try someone else.'

His weary sigh elicited some sympathy in Jess. 'I've already tried every other hire car company on the Central Coast,' he said. 'Look, are you absolutely certain you can't wangle something? I don't need a limo or anything fancy. Any car and driver would do. I have to be in Mudgee for a wedding on Saturday, not to mention the stag party tomorrow night. The groom's my best friend and I'm the best man. But a drunk driver ran into me last night, wrecked my rental and left me unable to drive myself. I've a bunged up right shoulder.'

'That's terrible.' Jess hated drivers who drank. 'I truly wish I could help you, sir.' Which she genuinely did. It would be awful if he couldn't make it to his best friend's wedding.

'I'm prepared to pay over and above your normal rates,' he offered just as she was about to suggest he try one of the larger hire car firms in Sydney. They could surely send a car up to him lickety-split. He might even have success hiring an ordinary taxi.

'How much over and above?' she asked, thinking of the hefty repayments she had to make on her SUV.

'If you get me a car and driver, you can name your own price.'

Wow, Jess thought. This American had to be loaded. He could probably afford to charter a helicopter—not that she was going to suggest such a thing. Jess wasn't about to look a gift horse in the mouth.

'Okay, Mr...er...?'

'De Silva,' he said.

Jess's mouth dropped open.

'Benjamin De Silva,' he elaborated.

Jess's mouth remained agape as she took in this amazing coincidence. With his being American and having such a distinctive name, he *had* to be the same man!

'Are you still there?' he finally asked after twenty seconds of shocked silence.

'Yes, yes, I'm still here. Sorry, I...er...was distracted for a moment. The cat just walked onto my keyboard and I lost a file.' In actual fact, the family moggie was sound asleep on a sun-drenched window sill, a good ten metres away from Jess's desk.

'You have a *cat* in your office?'

He actually sounded appalled. No doubt there were no cats allowed in the pompous Mr De Silva's office.

'This a home-run business, Mr De Silva,' she said somewhat stiffly.

'I see,' he said. 'Sorry. No offence intended. So, can you help me or not?'

Well, of course she could help him. And it was no longer just a question of money. For how could she possibly give up the opportunity to tell the high and mighty Mr Benjamin De Silva what was wrong with Fab Fashions?

Surely there would be plenty of opportunities somehow to bring up her lost job during the course of their very long drive together. Mudgee was a long way away. She'd never actually been there but she'd seen it on the map when she and Colin had been planning their trip. It was a large country town in the central west of New South Wales, a good five- or six-hour drive from here, maybe longer, depending on the state of the roads and the number of times her passenger wanted to stop.

'I can take you myself, if you like,' she offered. 'I am well over twenty-one, a qualified mechanic and an advanced driving instructor.' She only helped out in the office on Mondays and Thursdays. 'I also own a brand-new four-wheel drive which won't have any trouble negotiating the roads out Mudgee way.'

'I'm impressed. And extremely grateful.'

And so you should be, she thought a little tartly.

'So where exactly are you now, Mr De Silva? I'm presuming you're on the Central Coast somewhere.'

'I'm staying in an apartment at Blue Bay.' He gave her the address.

Jess frowned as she tapped it into the computer, wondering why a businessman like him would be staying up here instead of in Sydney. It seemed odd. Maybe he was just doing the tourist thing whilst he was in the country. Combining business with pleasure, as well as going to his best friend's wedding.

'And the address in Mudgee where I'll be taking you?' she asked.

'It's not actually *in* Mudgee,' he replied. 'It's a property called Valleyview Winery, not far from Mudgee. It's not difficult to find. It's on a main road which connects the highway to Mudgee. After you drop me off, you could stay at a motel in Mudgee till I need you to drive me back here again on the Sunday. At my expense, of course.'

'So you won't actually need me to drive you anywhere on the Saturday?'

'No, but I'll pay you for the day just the same.'

'This is going to be ridiculously expensive, Mr De Silva.'

'I'm not worried about that. Name your price and I'll pay it.'

Jess pulled a face. It must be nice never having to worry about money. She was tempted to say some exorbitant amount but of course she didn't. Her father would be appalled at her if she did such a thing. Joe Murphy was as honest as the day was long.

'How about a thousand dollars a day, plus expenses?' Mr De Silva suggested before she could calculate a reasonable fee.

'That's too much,' she protested before she could think better of it.

'I don't agree. It's fair, under the circumstances.'

'Fine,' she said briskly. Who was she to argue with Mr Moneybags? 'Now, I will need some other details.'

'Like what?' he demanded in a rather irritated tone.

'Your mobile phone number,' she said. 'And your passport number.'

'Okay. I'll have to go get my passport. I won't be long.'

Jess smiled whilst he gathered the information he wanted. Three thousand dollars was a very nice sum.

'Here we are,' he said on returning, and read out the number.

'We also need a contact name and number,' she said as she typed in the details. 'In case of an emergency.'

'Good grief. Is all this strictly necessary?'

'Yes, sir,' she said, wanting to make sure he was the right man. 'Company rules.'

'Fine. My father will have to do. Mum's on a cruise. But Dad does live in New York.'

'I did assume he'd be American, Mr De Silva. You have an American accent. His name and number, please?'

'Morgan De Silva,' he said and Jess smiled. She'd *known* it had to be him!

He rattled off a phone number which she quickly typed in.

'Do you want to pay for this via your credit card or cash?' she asked crisply.

'Which would you prefer?'

'Credit card,' she said.

'Fine,' he said, a decided edge creeping into his voice. 'I have it here.'

He read out the number. American Express, of course.

'Okay. That's all done. We'll deduct one thousand dollars in advance and the rest on completion.'

'Fine,' he bit out.

'What time would you like me to pick you up tomorrow morning, Mr De Silva?'

'What time do you suggest? I'd like to be out there by mid-afternoon. But first, could we dispense with the "Mr De Silva" bit? Call me Benjamin. Or Ben, if you'd prefer.'

'If you like,' she said, slightly taken aback by this offer. Australians were quick to be on a first-name basis but she'd found people from other countries weren't quite so easy going. Especially those who were wealthy. Maybe Mr De Silva wasn't as pompous as she'd originally thought.

'As to time,' she went on with a little less starch in her own voice, 'I would suggest that I pick you up at seven-fifteen. That way we'll avoid the worst of the traffic. Any earlier and we'll run into the tradies plus Sydney commuters. Any later and it'll be the people going to work at Westfield's, not to mention the mothers taking their kids to school.' Lord, but she was babbling on a bit. She could almost hear him sighing down the line.

'Seven-fifteen it is, then,' he said abruptly as soon as

she gave him the opportunity to speak. 'I'll be waiting outside so we don't waste time.'

Jess's eyebrows lifted. She'd picked up a few well-heeled tourists in her time and they rarely did things like that. They always made her knock, were often late and never helped her with their luggage—if it was a trip to the airport, that was, and not just a day out somewhere.

'Excellent,' she said. 'I won't be late.'

'Perhaps you should give me *your* mobile phone number, just in case you don't show up for reasons outside your control.'

Jess rolled her eyes. It sounded like he was another subscriber to Murphy's Law. But what the heck? She was used to it.

'Very well.' And she rattled off her number.

'And what should I call *you*, Miss…er…?'

'Murphy. Jessica Murphy.' She was about to say he could call her Jess—everyone else did—but simply couldn't bring herself to be that friendly to him. He was still the enemy, after all.

So she said a businesslike goodbye instead and hung up.

CHAPTER TWO

BEN SIGHED AS he flipped his phone shut and slipped it into his jeans pocket. The last thing he wanted to do was be driven all the way to Mudgee tomorrow by Miss Jessica Murphy, qualified mechanic and advanced driving instructor, he thought grumpily as he headed for the drinks cabinet. She'd declared herself well over twenty-one. More likely well over forty. And plain as a pikestaff to boot!

Still, what choice did he have after that doctor at Gosford hospital had declared him unfit to drive for at least a week? Not because of the excuse he'd given over the phone just now. His right shoulder *was* stiff and bruised but quite usable. It was the concussion he'd suffered which was the problem, the doctor having explained that no insurance company would cover him till he had a signed medical clearance.

Stupid, really. He felt fine. A little tired and frustrated, maybe, but basically fine.

Ben scowled as he sloshed a good two inches of his mother's best bourbon into one of her crystal glasses. He supposed he should be feeling grateful he'd found a hire car at all, not irritated. But Miss Jessica Murphy had got right up his nose. There was a fine line between efficient and officious and she'd certainly been straddling it. He half-regretted making the offer for her to call him Ben, but he'd had to do something to warm the old tartar up, otherwise the drive tomorrow would be worse than tedious.

If only his mother had been here, Ben thought as he headed for the kitchen in search of ice. She could have driven him. But she wasn't. She was off on a South Pacific cruise with her latest lover.

Admittedly, this one was older than her usual. In his mid-fifties, Lionel was only a few years Ava's junior. And he was currently employed—something in movie production—so he was a big improvement on the other fortune-hunting toy-boys who'd graced her bed over the years since his parents' divorce.

Not that his mother's affairs bothered him much these days. Ben had finally grown up enough to know his mother's personal life was none of his business. A pity she didn't return the favour, he thought as he scooped a few cubes of ice from the fridge's automatic ice-dispenser and dropped them in his glass. She was always asking him when he was going to get married and give her grandchildren.

So maybe it was better she wasn't here right now. The last thing he wanted was outside pressure about his relationship with Amber. He was having enough trouble as it was, deciding whether he should give up the romantic notion of marrying for love and settle for what Amber was offering. At least if he married Amber he wouldn't have to worry about her being a fortune hunter, which was always a problem when a man was heir to billions. Amber was the only daughter of a very wealthy property developer, so she didn't need a meal ticket in a husband.

In all honesty, Ben hadn't been under the impression that Amber wanted a husband at all yet. She was only twenty-four and was clearly enjoying her life as a single girl with a glamorous though empty job at an art gallery, a full social calendar and a boyfriend who kept her sexu-

ally satisfied. But, just before his trip down under, Amber
had suddenly asked Ben if he was ever going to propose.
She said she loved him, but she didn't want to waste any
more time on him if he didn't love her back and didn't want
marriage and children.

Of course he hadn't been able to tell her that he loved
her back, because he didn't. He'd said that he liked her a
lot but did not love her. Ben had been somewhat surprised
when she'd replied that she would be happy enough with
his liking her a lot. He'd assumed—wrongly, it seemed—
that a woman genuinely in love would be more heartbroken by his own lack of love. Apparently not! She'd given
him till Christmas to make up his mind. After that, she
would be looking elsewhere for a husband.

Ben lifted the bourbon to his lips as he wandered back
into the living room and over to the glass wall which overlooked the beach. But he wasn't really looking at the ocean
view. He was recalling how he'd told Amber that he would
think about her offer whilst he was in Australia and give
her an answer on his return.

And he *had* been thinking. A lot. He did want marriage
and children. *One* day. But, hell, he was only thirty-one.
On top of that, he wanted to feel more for his future wife
than he currently felt for Amber. He wanted to fall deeply
in love, and vice versa, the kind of love you had no doubts
over. The kind which would last. Divorce was not on his
agenda. Ben knew first-hand how damaging divorce was
to children, even when the parents were civilised about it,
as his own parents had been. His workaholic father had
sensibly and generously given Ben's mother full custody
of Ben, allowing her to bring him back to Australia, with
the proviso that Ben spent some of his school holidays
with him in America.

Ben had still been devastated to find out that his parents

no longer loved each other. He'd only been eleven at the time, and totally ignorant of the circumstances which had led to the divorce. It was testament to his parents' mutual love of their son that they'd never criticised each other in front of him, never blamed each other for the break-up of the marriage. They'd both just said that sometimes people fell out of love and it was better that they live apart.

Ben had hated coming to Australia at first, but he eventually grew to love this wonderful laid-back country and his life out here. He'd loved the school he'd been sent to and the many friends he'd made here. He'd especially loved his years at Sydney University, studying law and flat-sharing with Andy, his very best friend. It wasn't till he'd graduated that his father had finally told him the ugly truth: that his mother had trapped him into marriage by getting pregnant. She'd never loved him. She'd just wanted a wealthy husband. Yes, he'd also admitted to having been unfaithful to her, but only after she'd confessed the truth to him one night.

His father had claimed he hated hurting Ben with these revelations but believed it was in his best interests.

'You are going to inherit great wealth, son,' Morgan De Silva had said at the time. 'You need to understand the corrupting power of money. You must always keep your wits about you, especially when it comes to women.'

When a distressed Ben had confronted his mother, she'd been furious with his father, but hadn't denied she'd married the billionaire for his money, though she'd done her best to explain why. Born dirt-poor but beautiful, she'd had a tough childhood but had finally made it as a model in Australia and then overseas, having been taken on by a prestigious New York agency. For several years she'd made very good money but just before she'd turned thirty she'd discovered that her manager hadn't invested her money wisely, as she'd believed, instead having wasted it all on gambling.

Suddenly, she'd been close to broke again and, whilst she'd still been very beautiful, her career hadn't been what it once was. So, when the super-wealthy Morgan De Silva had come on the scene, obviously infatuated with the lovely Australian blonde, she'd allowed herself to be seduced in more ways than one. She'd been attracted to him, she'd insisted, but had admitted to Ben that she didn't love his father, saying she doubted he'd loved her either. It had just been a case of lust.

'The only thing your father loves,' she'd told Ben with some bitterness, 'is money.'

Ben had argued back that this wasn't true. His father loved *him*. Which belief had prompted his move to America shortly after his graduation from university.

Not that he'd cut his mother out of his life altogether. She'd been a wonderful mother to him and he still loved her, despite her faults and flaws. They talked every week or so on the phone, but he didn't visit all that often, mostly because he rarely had the time.

Life since going to the States had been full-on. An economics post-graduate degree at Harvard had been followed by an intense apprenticeship in the investment business. There'd been a few snide remarks when he'd made his way quickly up the ladder at De Silva & Associates, but Ben believed he'd earned his promotion to an executive position in his father's company, along with the seven-figure salary, the sizeable bonuses, the flash car and the equally flash New York apartment. Along the way, he'd also earned the reputation for being a bit of a playboy, perhaps because his girlfriends didn't last all that long. Invariably, after a few weeks he would grow bored with them and move on.

Never once had he fallen in love, making him wonder if he ever would.

It was a surprise to Ben that his relationship with Amber had lasted as long as it had—eight months—possibly because he didn't see all that much of her. He was working very long hours. He'd never thought himself in love with her. She was, however, attractive, amusing and very easy to be with, never fussing when he was late for a date or when he had to opt out at the last minute. Never acting in that clinging, possessive way which he hated.

She'd also never once said she loved him in all those months, so her recent declaration had come out of the blue.

Ben had been startled at first, then flattered, then tempted by her proposal, possibly because of his father's mantras, on marriage.

'Rich men should always marry rich girls,' he'd said more than once, along with, 'Rich men must marry with their heads. Never their hearts.'

Sensible advice. But it was no use. Ben knew, deep down in *his* heart, that marriage to a girl he didn't love would be settling for less than he'd always wanted. A lot less.

So his answer had to be no.

Ben considered ringing Amber and telling her so immediately, but there was something cowardly about breaking up over the phone or, God forbid, by text message. She'd already asked him not to call or text her whilst he was away, perhaps hoping that he would miss her more that way.

Frankly, just the opposite had happened. Without phone calls and text messages, the connection between them had been broken. Now that he'd made his final decision, Ben felt not one ounce of regret. Just relief.

When his phone suddenly vibrated in his pocket, Ben hoped like hell it wasn't Amber. But it wasn't her, the caller

ID revealing it was his father. Ben frowned as he lifted the phone to his ear. It wasn't like his father to call him unless there was a business problem. Morgan De Silva wasn't into social chit-chat.

'Hi, Dad,' Ben said. 'What's up?'

'Sorry to bother you, son, but I was thinking about you tonight and decided to give you a call.'

Ben could not have been more taken aback.

'That's great, Dad, but shouldn't you be asleep? It must be the middle of the night over there.'

'It's not that late. Besides, you know I never sleep much. What time is it where you are?'

'Mid-afternoon.'

'What day?'

'Thursday.'

'Ah. Right. So you'll be off to Andy's wedding in a couple of days.'

'I'm actually driving up to his place tomorrow.' For a split second Ben contemplated telling his father about the accident and his fiasco about finding a hire car, but decided not to. Why worry him unnecessarily?

'Nice boy, Andy.'

His father had met Andy when Ben had brought him to America for a holiday. They'd gone skiing with Morgan and had a great time.

'So, when do you think you'll be back in New York?' his father asked.

'Probably not till the end of next week. Mum's away on a cruise and doesn't get back till next Monday. I'd like to spend a day or two with her before I fly home.'

'Of course. Why don't you stay a little longer? Have a decent holiday? You deserve it. You've been working way too hard.'

Ben stared out at the beach and the ocean beyond. In

truth, it had been a couple of years since he'd had more than a long weekend off, his mother recently having accused him of becoming a workaholic, just like his father.

'I might do that,' he said. 'Thanks, Dad.'

'My pleasure. You're a good boy. Give my regards to your mother,' his father said abruptly, then hung up.

Ben stared down at his phone, wondering what in the hell that had been all about.

CHAPTER THREE

JESS WAS GLAD to get out of the house the following morning before her parents were up and about. Her mother had
started going on and on the night before about her taking
a risk, driving some stranger all the way out to Mudgee
and back.

'He might be a serial killer for all you know,' she'd said
at one stage.

She hadn't stopped with the doomsday scenarios till
Jess had told her everything she knew about Mr Benjamin De Silva, including his being the son of a super-rich
American businessman whose company had taken over
several Australian firms, including Fab Fashions.

'He's not a serial killer, Mum,' she'd informed her
mother firmly. 'Just a man with more money than sense.'

To Jess's surprise, her sometimes pessimistic father had
taken her side in the argument.

'Jess knows how to look after herself, Ruth,' he'd said.
'She'll be fine. Just give us a call when you get there, love,
and put your mother's mind at rest. Okay?'

She'd happily agreed to do so, but hadn't trusted her
mum not to start up again this morning, so she'd packed
an overnight bag the night before, then risen early, giving her time to take some extra care getting ready. Under
the circumstances, she didn't want to look like a dag. Or

a chauffeur, for that matter—so she'd already dismissed
the idea of wearing her usual driving uniform of black
trousers with a white shirt which had *Murphy's Hire Car*
emblazoned on the breast pocket.

She did wear black trousers. Rather swish, stretchy
ones which tapered in at the ankles and made the most
of her long legs, combining them with a V-necked white
T-shirt topped with a floral jacket which she'd made herself. Jess was an excellent dressmaker, having been taught
how to sew by her gran. She dithered a bit over how much
make-up to wear, opting in the end to play it conservative,
using just a bit of lip gloss and a light brushing of mas-
cara. Her clear olive skin did not really need foundation,
anyway. She then scooped her thick, black hair back up
into a ponytail, wrapping a red scrunchie around it which
matched the red flowers in the jacket. Finally, she pulled
on a pair of very comfy black pumps before bolting out
of the house by six-thirty, a good twenty minutes before
she needed to leave.

The drive from Glenning Valley to Blue Bay would take
fifteen minutes at most. Probably less at this time of day.
She filled in some time having breakfast at a local burger
bar, after which she drove leisurely towards the address
she'd been given. Jess knew the area well. Whilst there
were still lots of very ordinary weekenders around, any
property on the beach front was worth heaps. Most of the
older buildings which had once graced the shoreline had
been torn down, replaced by million-dollar units and multi-
million-dollar homes. Over the last decade, Blue Bay had
become one of *the* places to live on the coast.

It wasn't till she turned off the Entrance Road into the
long street which led down to Blue Bay that Jess felt the
first inkling of nerves. Though normally a confident and
rather outspoken girl, she suddenly realised it wasn't going

to be easy bringing up the subject of Fab Fashions with the man responsible for taking over the company. If truth be told, he would probably tell her to mind her own business. He also wouldn't be pleased with the fact that she'd looked him up on the Internet.

Maybe she should forget about the probably futile idea of trying to save Fab Fashions and just do what Mr De Silva had hired her to do—drive him out to Mudgee and back. Alternatively, maybe she would wait and see what kind of man he was; if he was the kind to listen or not. He hadn't sounded too bad over the phone. Maybe a little frustrated, which was understandable, considering he'd just had a car accident and all his plans had gone awry. And he *had* asked her to call him Ben, which was rather nice of him. She almost felt guilty now that she hadn't asked him to call her Jess in return.

Jess wondered how old he was. Probably about forty, she guessed. If he looked anything like his father—there'd been a photo of Morgan De Silva on the Net—then he'd be short, with a receding hairline and a flabby body from a sedentary lifestyle and too many long business lunches.

'Oh, dear,' she sighed.

Jess was no longer looking forward to today in any way, shape or form.

After letting out the breath she'd been unconsciously holding, she started scanning the numbers on the post boxes, soon realising that the number she was looking for would be on the left and right down the end of the street. Truly, what else had she expected? The son of a billionaire wouldn't be staying anywhere but the best.

The sun was just rising as she approached a block of apartments which carried the right number and which, yes, of course, overlooked the beach. A man was already standing on the pavement outside the building. Beside him sat a black travel case on wheels, across which was draped a plastic zip-up suit bag.

Jess tried not to stare as she pulled into the kerb beside him. But it was difficult not to.

He wasn't short with a receding hairline and flabby body. Hell, no. He was anything but. He was very tall and slim, with broad shoulders and the kind of well-chiselled face you saw on male models in magazines advertising aftershave or expensive watches. High cheekbones, a strong, straight nose and a square jawline. His hair was a light sandy colour, cut short at the sides and slightly longer on top, brushed straight back from that oh, so handsome face. His skin was lightly tanned, his eyes blue and beautiful. His clothes were more what she'd been expecting. Sort of. Dark-grey trousers and a long-sleeved blue business shirt which was open at the neck and which had a pair of sunglasses tucked into the breast pocket.

Jess dragged her eyes away from him, switched off the engine, then climbed out of the car, her thoughts somewhat scattered. Who would have imagined he would be so good-looking? Or so *young*? He couldn't be more than early thirties. Maybe even younger.

'Mr De Silva, I presume?' she asked as she stepped up onto the pavement less than a metre from him. Up close, he was even more attractive, if that were possible.

'You can't possibly be Miss Murphy,' he returned, the hint of a wry smile teasing one corner of his nicely shaped mouth.

She bristled at his comment. 'I don't see why not.'

He shook his head as he looked her up and down. 'You're not what I was expecting.'

'Oh?' she returned stiffly. 'And what were you expecting?'

'Someone a little older and a little less…er…attractive.'

Jess thanked the Lord she wasn't a blusher. For if she had been she might have gone bright red under the openly admiring gaze of those beautiful blue eyes.

'That's nice of you to say so, Mr De Silva. I think,' she added, wondering if she'd sounded old and ugly on the phone.

'I told you to call me Ben,' he said, and smiled at her, a full hundred-watt smile which showed perfect American teeth and a charm which was just as dazzling.

Oh my, Jess thought, trying not to be too dazzled.

Not without much success, given she just stood there staring at him whilst her heartbeat did the tango and she forgot all about Fab Fashions.

'Perhaps we should get going,' he said at last.

Jess gave herself a mental shake. It wasn't like her to go ga-ga over a man, even one as impressive as this.

'Yes. Yes, of course,' she said, still far too breathlessly for her liking. 'Do you need help with your bags?' she added, recalling what he'd said about having a banged-up right shoulder.

'I can manage,' he returned. 'Just open up the back for me.'

He managed very well. Managed the passenger door without any help either.

By the time she climbed into the driving seat and belted up, Jess had taken control of her wildly dancing heartbeat, having told herself firmly to get a grip and stop acting like some awestruck schoolgirl. She was twenty-five years old, for pity's sake!

Taking a deep breath, she reached for her sunglasses and put them on.

'Would you mind if I called you Jessica instead of Miss Murphy?' he said before she could even start the engine.

Jess winced. She hated being called Jessica. 'I'd rather

you call me Jess,' she replied, and found herself throwing a small smile his way.

'Only if you promise to call me Ben,' he insisted as he snapped his seat belt into place.

Jess suspected that women—no, people in general—rarely said no to Ben De Silva. His combination of looks and charm were both seductive and quite corrupting. Already she wanted to please him. Yet she wasn't, by nature, a people pleaser. Jess had always had a mind of her own and a mouth to match. Suddenly, however, all she wanted to do was smile, nod and agree with everything Ben said. Already he was Ben in her head.

'Okay. Ready, Ben?' she said as she reached for the ignition and glanced over at him again.

Dear heaven but he *was* gorgeous! He smelt gorgeous too. She did like men who wore nice aftershave.

'As soon as I put these on,' he replied, pulling his own sunglasses out of his pocket.

They were very expensive looking. God, now he looked like a movie star, a very sexy movie star, the kind a girl fantasised over in the privacy of her bedroom.

Jess's susceptibility to this man was beginning to annoy her. Next thing she'd know, she'd start flirting with him. Which wasn't like her at all! Gritting her teeth, she checked her rear and side mirrors, executed a perfect three-point turn, then accelerated up the street. Neither of them said anything for a full minute or two, Ben being the first to speak.

'I must thank you again, Jess, for doing this for me.'

'You don't have to thank me. You're paying for the privilege.'

'Still, I can see you probably had to put yourself out to do this. I would imagine a girl as attractive as yourself would have better things to do over the weekend than work.'

'No, not really.'

'You didn't have to break any dates?'

'Not this weekend.'

'That surprises me. I would have thought you'd have a boyfriend.'

'I did,' she bit out. 'Till recently.'

'What happened?'

She shrugged. 'We were going to go on a road trip together around Australia. That's why I bought this four-wheel drive. Anyway, at the last moment he decided he didn't want to do that. Instead, he took off backpacking around the world with a mate.'

Jess felt, rather than saw, Ben's startled look. When driving a client, she rarely took her eyes off the road.

'He didn't ask you to go with him?' he quizzed, his shocked tone soothing Jess's still lingering hurt over Colin's defection.

'No. He did ask me to wait for him, though.'

'I hope you said no.'

She laughed as she recalled her quite volatile reaction. 'I said a little more than just no.'

'Good for you.'

'Perhaps. Colin said I have a sharp tongue.'

'Really? I find that hard to believe.'

Was he mocking her?

A quick glance showed a perfectly straight face. A perfectly straight, very handsome face. Jess decided he was just making conversation, which was better than sitting there saying nothing all the way to Mudgee.

'He also said I was bossy and controlling.'

'No!'

He *was* mocking her. But not unkindly.

She sighed. 'I suppose I am a bit controlling. But I just like things to be organised. And to be done properly.'

'I'm somewhat of a perfectionist myself,' Ben said. 'Ah, there's Westfield's. Not far to the motorway now.'

Jess frowned. 'How come you know Westfield's? I thought this was your first visit to Australia.'

'Not at all,' he said. 'I've spent a lot of time here. Well, in New South Wales, at least. My parents are divorced, you see. You already know my father's American, but my mother's Australian. She owns the apartment in Blue Bay. I actually went to boarding school in Sydney. That's where I met Andy—he's the one who's getting married.'

'Goodness!' she exclaimed. 'I had no idea.'

'Well, why would you?' he said, sounding puzzled.

Jess suppressed a groan. As the saying went, *oh, what a tangled web we weave when first we practise to deceive.*

It actually went against Jess's grain to be less than honest with people. But her intentions had been good. Hopefully, Ben wouldn't be too annoyed with her if she told him the truth. She really didn't want to drive all the way to Mudgee watching what she said and didn't say. And, yes, she supposed she did still hope to discuss the future of Fab Fashions with him. He seemed very approachable and a lot smarter than she'd given him credit for. But that didn't make the act of confessing any easier.

'Oh gosh, this is just so awkward. I suppose I simply *have* to tell you now. I…I just hope you won't be too annoyed.'

CHAPTER FOUR

BEN HAD NO idea what she was talking about. 'Tell me what?' he asked.

'The thing is, Ben…' she started, obviously with great reluctance.

'Yes?' he prompted when she didn't go on.

She pulled a face. 'I just hope you understand.'

'Understand *what*?' he demanded to know.

'Just wait, will you, till we're safely on the motorway?'

Jess turned right onto the ramp which took them down to the highway, heading north.

'I have a confession to make,' she said at last, then hesitated again.

'Go on,' Ben said with more patience than he was feeling.

'The thing is… I knew who you were yesterday on the phone once you said you were Benjamin De Silva.'

Ben tried to assimilate what Jess was actually saying, but failed.

'What exactly do you mean by who I was?'

'I mean, I knew you worked for De Silva & Associates and that you were Morgan De Silva's son.'

Ben could not have been more taken aback.

'And how come you knew that?' he said, sounding more confused than angry. 'I wouldn't have thought my father was all that well known in Australia. He keeps a low public profile. Same with myself.'

Her sigh was heavy. 'You might understand better if I tell you I used to have a part-time job at a Fab Fashions boutique in Westfield's till last weekend, when the manager had to let me go.'

'Ah,' Ben said, light dawning. Though what she was doing working part-time in a fashion boutique at all was a mystery. She'd said she was a mechanic, hadn't she? And an advanced driving instructor.

There was no doubt that Jess was a surprising girl in more ways than one. You could have knocked him over with a feather when she'd turned up, looking nothing like the middle-aged battle-axe he'd been envisaging. Not only was she young—surely no more than mid- to late-twenties—she was also hot looking. Normally he went for blondes, not brunettes. But he found Jess quite delicious with her full lips, flashing dark eyes and seriously great legs. She also had an engaging and rather amusing personality. That boyfriend had been a fool, letting her go.

'Yes, ah…' Jess said somewhat sheepishly. 'I asked Helen…she's the manager…what the problem was and she told me about this American company taking over Fab Fashions and threatening them with closure if they didn't make a profit before the end of the year. I was so mad I found out what your name was and looked you up on the Internet. Not that I found out much about you,' she added hastily. 'Mostly it was about your father and the company he founded. Anyway, when an American chap rang yesterday and told me his name was Benjamin De Silva, I nearly fell off my chair.'

Ben didn't doubt it.

'So why on earth did you agree to drive me anywhere?'

he asked her. 'I would have thought you would have told me to drop dead.'

'Good heavens, no. What would have been the point of that? Look, the truth is that I had this crazy idea that during our long drive out to Mudgee I could somehow bring Fab Fashions into the conversation. I imagined you'd be surprised at the coincidence that I'd once worked for them but that you wouldn't be suspicious. I'd then tell you what I thought could be done to make Fab Fashions more profitable. I know that sounds terribly arrogant of me but I do know fashion. It's a lifelong passion with me. My grandmother was a professional seamstress and she taught me everything she knew. I've also done a design course online and I make a lot of my own clothes.'

'I see,' Ben said slowly. She was serious, he realised, but truly there was probably no saving Fab Fashions. Retail was in a terrible shape worldwide. He'd only given them till the end of the year because he hadn't wanted to play Scrooge. His father had wanted him to shut them down straight away, having bought them only because it came as a package deal along with other companies which had much better prospects and assets.

But Ben wasn't about to tell Jess that. Not yet, anyway.

'So why did you look so surprised when we first met today?' he asked, trying to get the full picture.

Jess frowned.

'You did stare at me, Jess,' he went on when she didn't say anything.

'Yes… Yes, I did, didn't I?' she said, seeming a little flustered. 'The thing is…there was a photo of your father on the Internet and…well…you don't look much like him, do you?'

Ben had to smile. She really didn't have a tactful bone in her body. Or maybe he meant artful. Yes, that was it. Jess was not, by nature, a deceiver. She was open and honest. He suddenly wished that something could be done with Fab Fashions, just to please her.

'No,' he agreed. 'I take after my mother.'

'She must be very beautiful.'

Ben suppressed another smile with difficulty. Lord, but she was quite enchanting. And totally ingenuous in her honesty. She wasn't trying to flatter him, or flirt with him. Which was a change. It was years since Ben had encountered a girl who did neither in his company.

'Mum was very beautiful when my father married her,' he said. 'She still is, despite being over sixty. She was quite a famous model in her time. But that came to an end when she married Dad. After their divorce, she came back to Sydney and started up a modelling agency. Did very well too. Sold it for heaps a couple of years back. But perhaps you already knew all that, did you? From the Internet?'

'Heavens, no. The only personal information was that your father was divorced with one son, Benjamin. The article was all about business. It didn't say a word about your mother.'

Ben imagined that was his father's doing. He was a powerful man and still very bitter about the divorce. He rarely spoke of his ex-wife, which made his parting words on the phone last night extremely surprising.

Give my regards to your mother...

Odd, that.

'Ben, I'm really very sorry for prying into your life like that,' Jess suddenly blurted out, perhaps interpreting his thoughtful silence for annoyance. 'I realised as soon as I met you that I shouldn't have done it. But I didn't mean any harm. Truly.'

'It's all right, Jess,' he said reassuringly. 'I haven't taken offence. I was just thinking about Fab Fashions,' he invented. 'And wondering what we could do about it. To-gether.'

'Oh,' she said, and fairly beamed over at him, her smile lighting up her face in a way which went beyond beauty.

It was a force of nature, that smile. He felt it deep down in his gut. Very deep down.

His flesh leapt and he thought, *Uh-oh. This is not what I need right now.*

And then he thought…why not? He'd finished with Amber. What was to stop him from exploring this attraction further?

Ben almost laughed. Because this wasn't just attraction he was suddenly feeling down south of the border. This was lust, an emotion he was not unfamiliar with. But this time it felt stronger. Much stronger.

Impossible to ignore.

Impossible not to pursue.

Though not too seriously. He'd be going back to America soon. All he could fit in was a short fling.

His conscience pricked him. Jess didn't come across as the kind of girl who indulged in short flings. Though, maybe he was wrong. Maybe she'd be only too willing to go along with whatever he wanted. After all, he was the son of a billionaire, wasn't he? That made him super-attractive to women. On top of that, she already thought him very beautiful.

'You'd honestly listen to what I have to say about Fab Fashions?' she asked him eagerly.

'I'd be mad not to,' he replied, since this would give him a viable excuse to spend more time with her whilst he was in Australia. 'You're obviously a clever girl, Jess, with lots of smarts.'

'I'm not all that smart,' she said with delightful self-deprecation.

'I don't believe that.'

'Look, there's smart and there's smart. School smart, I wasn't. But I've always been good with my hands.'

Ben wished she hadn't said that, his eyes drifting over to where her hands were wrapped around the steering wheel. Hell, but he wanted those hands wrapped around *him*. Caressing him, stroking him, teasing him, whilst she did delicious things with her mouth. Such thoughts sent hot blood roaring through his veins, giving him an instant and quite painful erection.

Ben gritted his teeth as he tried to will his aroused body back into line. He was not a man who liked tipping out of control, even sexually. *Especially* sexually. Ben liked to be the boss in the bedroom, or wherever it was he chose to have sex. He enjoyed having total control of the action, along with his partner, which meant he had to have total control over himself, something which he'd practised and perfected over the years.

'Is that why you became a mechanic?' he asked, pleased with how normal he sounded despite his wayward flesh continuing to defy him.

Her shrug showed surprising indifference to her choice of career. 'Before Dad started up his hire car business, he owned a garage. Not up here. Down in Sydney. Anyway, all my brothers became mechanics and I just followed suit.'

'So when did you move up to the Central Coast?'

'A good few years back now,' she replied. 'I'd just finished my apprenticeship. I know I had my twenty-first birthday party up here so I must have been nineteen or twenty. I'm not sure of the exact year. Why?'

'Just making conversation, Jess,' he said, searching his mind for more safe topics. He could not believe that he still had an erection. 'You're not using your GPS, I see. So I guess you know the way to Mudgee.'

'It's pretty straightforward. We stay on the motorway till we reach the New England Highway, heading for Brisbane. But we turn off onto the Golden Highway just before Singleton. Then we don't get off that road till the turn-off to Mudgee. Easy peasy.'

'You sound like you've been this way a dozen times before.'

'I've driven to Brisbane via the New England Highway once or twice but I've never been along the Golden Highway before. Or to Mudgee, for that matter. I checked it up last night on the Internet.'

'I've never been this way before either,' he admitted.

Her glance carried curiosity. 'You've never been to your best friend's place before?'

'Yes, of course I have. Several times. But you take a different route when you're driving from Sydney.'

'Oh yes, of course. I didn't think of that. You said you went to boarding school in Sydney, is that right?'

'Yes. Kings College. It's near Parramatta. Do you know it?'

CHAPTER FIVE

A MOMENTARY FLASH of pique had Jess's hands tightening around the steering wheel. Just because she'd said she wasn't school smart didn't mean she was ignorant. Of course she knew of Kings College. It was one of the best private schools in Sydney. Despite it being located in the western suburbs, it was a far cry from the humble high school she'd gone to only a few miles away.

'Yes. I know it,' she said, thinking how way out of her league this man was. 'It's a very good school.'

'That's where I met Andy.'

'Your best friend?'

'Yes. We went on to study law together at Sydney Uni as well.'

Oh, Lord. Now he'd studied law at Sydney University, another prestigious establishment. Jess knew what it took to get into law. Which showed Ben was very school smart. But then, she'd guessed that already.

What next? she wondered. He probably wintered in the ski fields of Austria every year. And took his girlfriend to Paris for romantic weekends.

This last thought gave her a real jolt. Jess hadn't thought of Ben as having a girlfriend, which was very stupid of her. Of course he must have, a man like him. Not a wife, though.

When she'd asked him for a contact name and number yesterday he hadn't mentioned a wife.

A fiancée was still on the cards, however.

'And now your best friend is getting married,' she said, trying to make her voice cool and conversational, not like she was dying of curiosity. 'Are *you* married, Ben?' she asked.

'No,' he said.

'Engaged?'

'No.'

She'd gone too far now to stop. 'You must have a girlfriend back home.'

'Not any more. I did have a girlfriend. But, like yours, that relationship has now gone by the board.'

'She *dumped* you?' Jess said with total disbelief in her voice.

'Not exactly…'

'Sorry. I'm prying again.'

'I don't mind,' he said. 'I enjoy talking to you. Actually, *I'm* the one who decided to call it quits. I just haven't had the opportunity to tell Amber yet. I only decided last night.'

Amber, Jess thought with a curl of her top lip. A typical name for the type of girl he would date. She sounded beautiful. And rich. Jess hated her, till she remembered Ben was breaking up with her. Since that was the case, she could afford to be less bitchy. But she was still curious.

'What went wrong?'

'She wanted marriage and I didn't.'

'I see,' she said. What was it with men these days that they shied away from commitment?

When Jess found herself surrendering to a sinking feeling, she decided a change of subject was called for. She thought of returning to the problems with Fab Fashions but for some strange reason her enthusiasm for that project had lost some of its appeal. It was probably a waste of time, anyway. So she turned to that old favourite to fill awkward moments in a conversation. The weather.

'I'm so glad it's a nice sunny day,' she said with false brightness. 'There's nothing I hate more than driving in the rain. Though the recent rain was greatly appreciated. We had a terribly dry winter. Now everything's lovely and green.'

Ben turned his head to gaze at the countryside. 'It does look good. I can't say the same for this road, though. It's deplorable for a main highway. All cracked and patched up.'

'That's because it's built over the top of coal mines,' Jess explained. 'It suffers from subsidence. Still, that's Australia for you. We're notorious for our dreadful roads.'

'That's because the country is too big for your population. Not enough taxes for proper infrastructure.'

'Not enough taxes!' Jess exclaimed, putting aside her uncharacteristic desire to please and giving vent to her usual outspokenness. 'We're one of the highest taxed countries in the world!'

'Not quite. Australia's only number ten. Most European countries pay higher taxes.'

'Not America, though,' Jess argued. 'People can become rich in America. It's hard to become rich in Australia unless you're a crook or a drug dealer. Though, come to think of it, bankers are doing pretty well at the moment,' she added a touch tartly. 'My dad works his bum off and still only makes a living. Mum and Dad haven't had a decent holiday in years.' She didn't call five days in Bali last year a decent holiday.

'That's a shame. Everyone must have holidays these days or stress will get you in the end.'

'That's what I keep telling them.'

'How old are they?'

'Dad's sixty-three. Mum's fifty-nine.'

'Close to retirement age, then.'

'Dad says he'd rather die than retire.'

'My dad says the same thing,' Ben said. 'He loves working.'

Loves making money, you mean, Jess thought but didn't say.

'You mentioned brothers earlier,' Ben said. 'How many do you have?'

'What? Oh…er…three.'

'I always wanted a brother. So, Jess, tell me a bit about these brothers of yours.'

Jess shrugged. There seemed no point not telling him about her family. They had to talk about something, she supposed.

'Connor's the oldest,' she said. 'He's thirty-six. Married with two boys. Then there's Troy. He's thirty-four and married too, with twin girls. They're eight,' she added, smiling as she thought of Amy and Emily, who were the sweetest girls. 'Then there's Peter, who's closest to me at twenty-seven. He's not long married and his wife is expecting a bub early next year.'

'No sisters?'

'No, no sisters.'

'So you're the baby of the family.'

'Not a spoilt one, I can assure you,' she said, though this was a lie. Her brothers had indulged her shamelessly. And had been very protective of her when the boys had started hanging around. They were the reason she hadn't had a boyfriend till she'd left school. Because they kept frightening them off. Peter, especially. Jess had been a virgin till she was close to twenty.

'I suppose you want kids as well. I saw you smiling when you talked about the twin girls.'

'I'd love at least two children,' Jess admitted. 'But getting married and having children is not high on my list of wants right now. I'm only twenty-five. First, I'd like to travel all around Australia. That's why I bought this little darling,' she added, tapping the steering wheel. 'Because it can cope with whatever terrible roads Australia can throw at me.

'Oh look, there's the turn-off to the Hunter Valley vineyards,' she pointed out. 'If you're staying up on the Central Coast for a while after you get back from your friend's wedding, then that's one of the places you should visit. It's lovely at this time of the year. Lots of great places to stay and terrific wine to taste. You can even go up in a balloon. Colin and I did that not long ago and it was fantastic.'

'Had you been going out with this Colin fellow for long?'

'Just over a year.'

'And you were serious about him?'

'Serious enough,' she admitted. 'To be honest, I thought I was in love with him. But I can see now that I wasn't.' How could she have been? Colin had been gone from her life less than a month and she already had the hots for another man.

'For what it's worth, Jess,' that other man said, 'I think this Colin was a total idiot, leaving a girl like you behind.'

Jess could not help glancing over at Ben. His head turned her way and their eyes would have met if they hadn't both been wearing sunglasses. Even so, something zapped between them like a charge of electricity, taking Jess's breath away. And suddenly she knew, as surely as she knew that she should get her eyes back on the road ahead quick smart, that Ben fancied her as much as she fancied him. And, whilst the realisation of his sexual interest was exciting and flattering, it also terrified the life out of her.

CHAPTER SIX

BEN COULD HARDLY contain the burst of triumph he experienced when he heard her sharply indrawn breath, then watched her reef her eyes back on the road like the hounds of hell were after her.

Perhaps they were, he thought darkly. Be damned with his conscience. Be damned with common sense! He had to have this girl. And soon.

Jess was annoyed with herself for feeling flattered by Ben's interest. Why shouldn't he fancy her? she reasoned with more of her usual self-confidence. She was an attractive girl, with a nice face and figure. And, yes, super legs. Okay, so she probably wasn't a patch on this Amber female, but *she* was over in New York and Jess was right here. On top of that, he didn't want Amber. *No, no, be honest here, Jess, it wasn't Amber he didn't want, just marriage.* No doubt he would have continued their sexual relationship if she hadn't put the hard word on him. The truth was he was out here in Australia, probably feeling a bit lonely, and suddenly there she was, with no boyfriend and availability written all over her stupid face!

Jess was dragged out of her frustrating train of thought by the sudden end of the motorway. She hadn't even seen the signs to slow down. Rolling her eyes at herself, she made a careful left at the roundabout onto the New England Highway and set sail for the Golden Highway. Thankfully, Ben had fallen silent. No doubt he was working out when to make a pass whilst she was working out how she was going to act when that happened.

As Jess drove on silently, she wondered why she couldn't be like other girls—the ones who could sleep with guys on a first date, or even on meeting them for the first time at a pub, or club, or disco or whatever. She could never do that. She found the idea repulsive. And dangerous. She had to get to know the guy first. And like him. Had to see that he liked her too. Liked her enough to wait for her. Till she felt ready to go all the way.

She'd made Colin wait for weeks. Jess suspected Ben wouldn't wait weeks for her.

Not that she wanted him to. Lord, what was happening to her here? This wasn't like her at all! But Ben wasn't like any man she'd ever met before. It wasn't just a question of his movie-star looks, although they were hard to ignore. There was something else. A cloak of confidence which he wore without effort and which she found incredibly attractive. And very sexy. He would be a fantastic lover, she was sure. Very experienced. Very…knowledgeable. He would know exactly what to do and how to do it to make sure she always came.

A shiver rippled down her spine at this last thought. She didn't always come during sex. But she would like to.

'When are we going to make our first stop?' Ben suddenly piped up. 'I'll need to have a coffee fairly soon.'

Jess suppressed a groan as she realised that she'd once again become distracted from her driving. It took an extreme effort of will to drag her overheated mind away from those corrupting thoughts and put it to the task of estimating exactly where they were, quickly realising that they couldn't be far from the turn-off onto the Golden Highway.

'Denman is about half an hour from here,' she said, having studied the route and memorised all the towns and services on the way. 'I checked it up on the Internet. It's a small historic town down in a valley with a nice pub and a couple of cafés. If that's too far off for you, we could drive into Singleton, but then we'd have to double back.'

'No. No doubling back. Denman sounds fine. You wouldn't happen to have any pain killers with you, would you? I should have taken a couple this morning but forgot.'

Jess only then remembered his bad shoulder. 'There's some in the glove box,' she said. 'And a bottle of water in your door, if you want to take the tablets straight away.'

'Thanks.'

'How bad is your shoulder?' she asked, happy to have something safe to talk about.

'It's a bit stiff and sore this morning, but honestly it's fine. I could have driven, but the doctor at the hospital said no. Not because of the shoulder—I had a mild concussion as well.'

'Best you didn't drive, then.'

'I'm glad I couldn't—I wouldn't have met you.'

Jess could not stop her heart swelling with pleasure. Yet she knew what he was about. She'd seen how her brothers had acted with girls whose pants they wanted to get into. She'd watched them lay the compliments on thick and fast. And she'd watched those silly girls lap them up, then give her brothers what they wanted in no time at all.

Maybe that was why *she'd* acted differently with boys who came onto her. Or she had, till this handsome devil had come along.

He'd thrown a spanner in her works all right. Jess

could not believe she was thinking of having a one-night stand with him. Or that just the thought of it made her heart race faster than a Formula One car on the starting blocks.

CHAPTER SEVEN

'WHAT A LOVELY little town this is,' Ben said.

They had stopped and were sitting at a table on the veranda of an old farmhouse which had been converted into a café, sipping their just-delivered coffee and looking out onto a quite lovely garden full of flowering shrubs. Ben knew nothing about gardening and plants but he knew what he liked. It was the same way with art. He never bought art on the so-called reputation of the artist. He only bought what he liked.

He glanced over the table at Jess and thought how much he liked her too. Maybe that was why his desire for her was so strong. During the last half-hour of the drive, he'd been thinking how he could be alone with her this weekend in a place suitable for seduction. And he'd finally come up with a plan which would work, provided she went along with the idea.

'So, Jess,' he said. 'I think it's about time you started telling me what's wrong with Fab Fashions. I didn't want to talk business during the drive; I just wanted to drink in the wonderful scenery. But now that we've stopped…'

She put down her cup, then looked up at him with those big brown eyes of hers, the kind of eyes a man could drown in. He almost wished she'd put her sunglasses back on. But she'd left them hooked over the sun visor in the four-wheel drive. Lord, but they were expressive eyes. He could only hope that his own didn't give away his innermost thoughts, since he'd removed his sunglasses a couple of minutes earlier and popped them back into his shirt pocket.

'You honestly want to hear my ideas?' she said, sounding somewhat sceptical.

Not really, he conceded privately. They were a waste of time. But it was part of his plan.

'But of course,' he said.

Her face lit up and, yes, so did her eyes. Guilt threatened, but he pushed it firmly aside. Guilt, Ben conceded, was no match for lust.

'Okay. Well, for starters there's its name. "Fab Fashions" implies it caters for the young where in fact most of the stock in Fab Fashions is targeted towards the more mature woman. Either change the name or change the stock. I would suggest change the name; there are enough clothes around for teenagers.

'Then you should change your buyers. Get people in who aren't just buying to price. Someone who knows what's in fashion and what is comfortable to wear. The more mature lady wants comfort as well as style. Also, it might be a good idea to stock more of the most common sizes instead of just buying across the board. Most women over forty are not size eight! And of course you *should* have an online store too. To fall behind the times is stupid.'

Ben was surprised and impressed. All her suggestions made sense. They might even work. 'You really know your stuff, don't you?'

'I told you…fashion is a genuine passion with me. On top of that, I hate to think of all those people losing their jobs. If every owner shut their stores during a down-turn in the economy, the country would go to the wall. Surely it's not always about profit, is it, Ben? I mean…everyone has to take the bad times with the good, especially big companies like yours.'

'It's not always quite as simple as that, Jess.'

She bristled. 'I knew you'd say that.'

'I didn't say I wasn't prepared to do what you suggested. What say we have a think over the weekend and see if we can find a fab new name which would lend itself to a successful marketing campaign?'

Jess's frown was instant. 'But we don't have any spare time this weekend. You have to go to a stag party tonight and the wedding's tomorrow. I suppose we could talk on the drive home.'

'We could,' he said. 'But when I'm excited about something, I like to get straight to it,' he added with considerable irony and another tweak to his conscience. 'How about I give Andy a ring and organise for you to stay at the winery over the weekend instead of some motel in Mudgee? They have a small cottage on the property away from the main house which is very comfy. We could stay there together.'

'Together!'

'There's two bedrooms, Jess. Of course, there won't be much time for talking tonight, since I'll be at Andy's bachelor party. But the wedding's not till four the next afternoon. That should give us plenty of time to talk. And, speaking of the wedding, I'm sure I could wangle you an invitation.' If she didn't have a suitable dress, he would take her into Mudgee and buy her one.

Wariness warred with temptation in her eyes. 'Won't Andy think it odd, you asking him to invite a virtual stranger to his wedding?'

'But you're not a stranger, Jess. I already know more about you than most of my past girlfriends. On top of that, we're now business colleagues. I'll tell Andy you're a marketing consultant I've hired to help me with Fab Fashions and who kindly offered to drive me up here after I had that unfortunate car accident. There's no need to mention anything about you working for a hire car company, is there?'

Jess shook her head. Did he honestly think she didn't know what he was doing? She wasn't a fool. But there was simply no saying no to him.

'You do like to take over, Ben, don't you?'

His smile was both charming and sexy at the same time. 'What can I say? People tell me I'm bossy and controlling.'

Jess laughed. He was a clever devil. But totally irresistible.

'I'm sure Andy's folks will still think it odd, you asking for us to stay together in that cottage.'

'In that case, I'll say we're dating.'

'But we're not!'

'We will be, come Sunday. I have every intention of asking you out once we get back to the coast.'

'I might say no.'

'Will you?'

'No.'

He grinned at her. 'Great. No problems, then. I'll tell Andy you're my new girlfriend.'

Jess sighed. 'You are incorrigible.'

'I'm smitten, that's what I am.'

She just stared at him. *She* was the one who was smitten. *He* just wanted to get into her pants.

'I think you should know in advance, Ben, that I don't sleep with a guy on a first date.' Or she hadn't, till he'd come along.

There was that hint of a smile again. 'Who said anything about sleeping?'

'Very funny. You know what I mean.'

'Yes, of course I do. Let me assure you, Jess, that I would always be respectful of your wishes.'

Mmm…meaning he was very confident that he could seduce her in no time flat. Which he could, of course. But she had to make some kind of stand. Her pride demanded it.

'Fine,' she said. 'Just so you understand my feelings in advance. I don't want to have to fight you off at the end of the night.'

'I appreciate you being straight with me, Jess. I admire honesty.'

Oh, dear. She hoped she didn't look too guilty. Because of course she was probably going to sleep with him. How could she possibly say no? He was the sexiest man she'd ever met.

'Soon as I finish this coffee, I'll ring Andy,' Ben said, looking very pleased with himself.

He made the call out of earshot, walking around the garden as he talked. Jess wondered what he was telling his friend. She hated to think it was one of those 'nudge-nudge, wink-wink, say no more' conversations where Ben and his best friend were becoming co-conspirators in her supposed seduction. She would hate that. Still, Andy had already to know that Ben hadn't been out here in Australia for long. So how could she possibly be a proper girlfriend? She was just someone he'd met and fancied, but who would be quickly forgotten once he flew back to America.

Now that she was thinking straight, Jess also doubted Ben would really do anything about Fab Fashions. His interest in her ideas was just a ploy to keep her sweet. It also crossed Jess's mind as she watched Ben chatting away to his friend that she wouldn't be the first girl he'd installed in that cottage for the weekend. He was the sort of guy who would always have a willing girl on his arm. And in his bed. Jess would just be one in a long line of conquests.

She didn't like that thought, or the other thoughts she'd been having since he'd left her at the table.

Feeling decidedly disgruntled, Jess stood up, thanked the lady who ran the café and marched back to her four-wheel drive.

CHAPTER EIGHT

AFTER BEN FINISHED his call to Andy, he went back to the table on the veranda, only to find it empty. He glanced around and saw that she was out by the SUV, standing with her arms crossed and her face not at all happy. Ben wondered what had gone wrong during the last ten minutes. And there he'd been, thinking all his plans for the weekend were on track. Andy had accepted his entire story about Jess and agreed to put them both in the cottage. He'd also said there would be no problem with her coming to the wedding tomorrow.

Her body language worsened as he walked towards her, her manicured but unvarnished fingertips digging into the sleeves of her floral jacket.

'What's wrong?' he asked straight away.

Her mouth tightened. 'I don't like lies, that's what's wrong! I'm not your girlfriend, Ben. Not really. Not yet, anyway. Why, you haven't even kissed me yet!'

Jess could not believe she'd just said that. It sounded dreadful, like she was *asking* him to kiss her.

'Well, that can be easily fixed,' he returned, his eyes dropping to her mouth as he reached out and took firm possession of her shoulders.

Oh, Lord, she thought as panic set in.

He didn't rush anything; her arms dropped to her sides

long before he actually kissed her. He gathered her against him very slowly, his eyes holding hers captive as easily as he was holding her body. The descent of his head was just as slow, Jess's heart pounding against her ribs by the time his lips made contact with hers. Even then, he didn't kiss her properly, just brushed his mouth over hers. Once. Twice. Three times. Finally, her tingling lips gasped apart, desperate for more.

But he denied her desire. And, in doing so, deepened it. She moaned when his head lifted, her eyes glazed as they stared up at him.

'Will that do for now to raise your status to girlfriend?' he said, shocking her with his cool manner. She was on fire inside. Yet he seemed totally unmoved.

'Like I said, lovely Jess,' he went on, 'I'm smitten with you. Seriously smitten. I'm already planning on extending my stay here in Australia to spend more time with you. And, since you don't like lies, let me say right here and now that I doubt very much if I can fix Fab Fashions, even with your very excellent ideas.'

He was a wicked devil, she decided shakily, using honesty now to seduce her.

'But I'm willing to give it a try,' he added, 'if it makes you happy.'

What to say to that? She could hardly admit that Fab Fashions wasn't high on her personal agenda right at this moment. All she could think about was being with this man.

At the same time, she didn't want Ben thinking he could play her for a fool.

Pulling herself together, Jess did her best to imitate his controlled demeanour.

'It would be nice to try to turn things around,' she said. 'So, yes, it would make me very happy.'

'Good. And, whilst I'm in the mood for confession,' he

went on, 'my reason for organising for us to stay together at the cottage was something far more…intimate.'

Ben was watching her eyes closely and decided she wasn't upset by his admission. Just the opposite, in fact. There was a glittering of dark excitement in their gorgeous depths. She was trying to act cool with him but her eyes gave her away. Besides, he'd felt her tremble in his arms just now. And that frustrated moan of hers had been very telling. She wanted him as much as he wanted her. He hadn't dared deepen that kiss for fear of losing it himself. Jess really did have a powerful effect on him. Much more than Amber ever had.

'Not tonight, unfortunately,' he said with true regret, 'Since I'll be otherwise occupied. But I thought by tomorrow night, after the wedding, I'd be in with a chance.'

'Did you now?' Jess threw at him, desperate to find some composure, not to mention her pride.

His beautiful blue eyes glittered with amusement, not to mention supreme confidence. 'Let's just say I was hopeful.'

'You'll need to improve your kissing technique.'

'Really? And there I was, thinking you'd enjoyed being teased.'

Jess shook her head in defeat. He was just too clever for her. And way too knowing. 'You are incorrigible.'

'And you're irresistible.'

Jess said nothing to that, but her mind kept ticking over. Oh yes, he was a wicked devil all right, with all the right words and all the right moves. She wondered how many women he'd had in his life.

Lots, she supposed.

And she would be just one more.

Not the happiest of thoughts.

'I think we should get going now,' she said abruptly. It

was almost ten; it had taken them longer to get to Denman than she'd estimated.

'Good idea,' he said.

They climbed in and belted up, both of them reaching for their sunglasses at the same time, Jess careful not to look over at him lest she give away even more of her vulnerability to this man. She hated Ben thinking he was onto a sure thing tomorrow night. Though, of course he was. No point in denying it to herself. But that didn't mean she had to act like some gushing nincompoop who was overwhelmed by his attentions.

'I thought we'd stop at Cassilis for lunch,' she said matter-of-factly as she started the engine. 'Sandy Hollow is the next town but it's too close. After that, it's straight to your friend's place.'

'Sounds like a good plan.'

'We should easily arrive by mid-afternoon, depending on how long you want to stop for lunch.'

'I guess that would depend on how quickly we get served.'

Very quickly, as it turned out. They settled on a pub lunch, eaten out in the very pleasant beer garden. Jess ordered just the one glass of white wine with her steak and salad, since she was driving, whilst Ben decided on a schooner of beer with his. But they ate slowly and talked a lot. And, whilst the conversation was very superficial, all the while Jess was aware of a dangerous excitement growing deep inside her. Every time she looked at Ben a sexual image jumped into her head. When he forked some food into his mouth, she found herself staring at that mouth and thinking of how it would feel kissing, not her mouth so much, but other more intimate parts of her body. His hands brought similar sexy images. They were rather elegant hands. Well-manicured with long fingers and rounded tips. Jess imagined them doing darkly delicious things to her.

Her bottom tightened with shock at her thoughts, for Jess was not that sort of girl. Or so she'd imagined up till now. Her boyfriends so far had been rather lacking in imagination when it came to foreplay, which was perhaps why she hadn't come every time. Not that she hadn't enjoyed herself. She liked male bodies, especially well-built ones. Sex with Colin had been somewhat better, perhaps because he liked her being on top. Which she liked too. Perhaps because of that controlling nature of hers, or because she always came that way.

Jess glanced over at Ben and wondered again how many women he'd had in his life. Which sent Amber into her mind.

Jess wished Ben had already broken up with her. She wanted to tell him to ring her and do it, right now! But she didn't have the courage—or the gall—to say so. It would be a waste of time, anyway. For what would it matter in the end? The cold, hard truth was that eventually he would leave her and go back to America anyway. He didn't want marriage. She was just a girl he'd met out here whom he fancied and whom he meant to have.

A part of Jess was flattered by his determined passion for her. But she didn't deceive herself into thinking this would ever be a serious romance. They were just ships passing in the night. She decided—perhaps in protection of her fluttering female heart—that she would think of him as an experience. An adventure. Possibly even an education. For Jess knew, as surely as she knew the house wine she was drinking was rubbish, that sex with Ben would be unlike anything she'd ever experienced before.

Falling for a man like Ben, however, would be a stupid thing to do. *Very* stupid.

'You've gone quiet on me,' Ben said.

Jess perked up immediately. She didn't want Ben to think she was worried about anything. Which she was, somewhat. But forewarned was forearmed. Now that she'd decided to go down this road, she was determined to do so in a positive state of mind. There were worse things that could happen to a girl than an affair with the handsome son of a billionaire. Not that Ben's having money mattered to her. Jess had never been overly impressed by wealthy people. They never seemed all that happy, for one thing. But Ben's privileged background had given him a confidence and polish which was very attractive.

'I was thinking I should ring Mum soon,' she said with a quick smile. 'And reassure her that I'm still alive.'

'What? Surely she wasn't worried about you driving? You're an excellent driver.'

'No. Mum has every faith in my driving abilities. She was worried that you might be a serial killer.'

The shock on his face was classic.

'I assured her that you weren't. You were just a rich businessman with not an ounce of intelligence to save your soul.'

He pretended to look offended. 'You *do* have a sharp tongue, don't you?'

His eyes narrowed as men did when they were challenged. 'I'm actually quite intelligent.'

'I've yet to see evidence of that fact.' Lord, but she was actually loving this. She'd never sparred verbally with Colin, or any of her other boyfriends. She'd never flirted like this either. But it was such fun.

'I'll have you know that I was dux of my school.'

'Yes, but that's just school smart, Ben, which is a lot different from street smart. How can you possibly be street smart when you were born with a silver spoon in your mouth?' It was a lovely mouth, though. The more she studied it, the more she liked it. His bottom lip was full and sensual, whilst his top lip was thinner and harder. She suspected Ben could be stubborn as well as arrogant. Maybe even a little ruthless. But there was something decidedly sexy about a man being ruthless. You wouldn't want to marry a ruthless man, but having an affair with him was a different matter entirely.

'Keep that up and your mother might have something to worry about,' he quipped, his beautiful blue eyes sparkling with good humour. 'Women have been strangled for less.'

She smiled, and was still smiling when they left the hotel and set off again. It wasn't till they were well down the road to Mudgee that she realised she *hadn't* rung her mother.

'Is this the road Andy lives on?' she asked.

'Yes, I'm sure it is.'

'Are we nearly there yet?'

'I think so. It's been a while since I've been up here but I'll recognise the place once I see it.'

'In that case I'd like to stop for a sec and make that phone call to Mum,' she said, pulling off the road and parking under the shade of a tree.

Her mother answered on the second ring.

'Jess?'

'Yes, Mum.'

'Are you okay? Are you there yet?'

'Yes, Mum, I'm almost there and I'm fine. Mr De Silva wasn't a serial killer after all,' she added, at which Ben shook his head at her. 'He's really quite nice,' she added, and pulled a face at him.

He smiled a crooked smile.

'That's a relief. A girl can't be too careful, you know.'

'Mr De Silva's friend lives at a winery along this road.

After I drop him off, I'll head into Mudgee and book into a motel. Look, I'd better go. I'll give you another call later tonight. Bye for now. Love you.'

'Why didn't you tell her you were staying at the winery?' Ben asked as she gunned the engine and pulled out onto the road. 'I thought you didn't like lies.'

'Don't be silly, Ben. She's my mother. All girls lie to their mothers. We do it to protect them from worry.'

He laughed. 'That's a good one. But I suppose it would be a bit hard to explain.'

'Very. Now, how far along this road is Valleyview Winery?'

'Not too far now. I recognise that place over there. I'm sure it's just along here on the left. Yes, there it is now.' And he pointed high up to the left.

Her eyes followed the direction of his finger, landing on an impressive federation-style homestead built on the crest of a hill so that its wraparound verandas could take advantage of the valley views.

'The driveway is not far now,' Ben added. 'Yes, there it is.'

Jess slowed, then turned into the driveway, passing through widely set stone gateposts, one of which doubled as a post box, the other having the name 'Valleyview Winery' carved into the stone and painted black so that it stood out. The driveway was relatively straight and nicely tarred, bisecting gently sloping paddocks which held rows and rows of grapevines.

'So, does this place belong to Andy or his parents?' she asked, Jess only then realising they hadn't really talked about Andy, or the upcoming wedding, at all. They'd been totally taken up with each other.

'His parents. And the house is actually not as old as it looks. His folks built it while we were at boarding school together. His dad was a stock broker in Sydney but made enough money to retire early, so he decided to indulge his hobby and start up a winery.'

Jess suppressed a sigh. She should have known Ben's best friend would be rich.

'And what does Andy do?'

'He's now the official wine-maker here. He did law like me when he first left school, but decided after we graduated that it wasn't for him, so he went to France and studied wine-making with the masters. Then he came back and took over. Till then his dad hired a professional wine-maker. Apparently, it's not an art you can learn from a how-to book.'

'I dare say.'

As they drew near to the house, three people emerged onto the front veranda. Two men and a woman. Jess presumed it was Andy and his parents. The younger of the two men separated himself from the others and hurried down some side steps which led to a large tarred area at the side of the house where she was about to park.

'This do?' she asked Ben as she pulled to halt.

'Perfect,' he said, already unclicking his seat belt. In no time he was out and hugging his best friend with a big bear-hug.

Andy wasn't as tall as Ben, she noted as she climbed out from behind the wheel, but he was nice looking, with dark hair, brown eyes and even features.

'Long time no see, bro,' Andy said, finally disengaging from the hug.

Ben shrugged. 'Been busy in the Big Apple.'

'You know what they say, mate, about all work and no play. Still, you're in Australia now, the land down under where the weather is hot and so are the girls. Speaking of hot girls, I presume this is Jess,' he added, giving her the once-over with appreciative eyes.

'How intuitive of you,' Ben mocked. 'Jess, this smart Alec is Andy.'

'Hi, there, Jess,' he said, and came forward to give her a peck on the cheek. 'Lovely to meet you.'

'Are you sure it's all right for me to stay here?' she said in reply. 'I wouldn't like to put your mother to any extra trouble.'

'No, no, she's fine with it. The cottage is always ready for guests and Mum's very easy going. Come inside and have some afternoon tea. And some of Mum's blueberry muffins—the ones you like, Ben. You know, Jess, I'm not sure what it is about Ben here, but women fuss over him like mad.'

'Search me,' she returned with a straight face. 'It's not as though he's handsome or charming or anything like that.'

Andy stared at her for a second, then laughed a big belly laugh. 'Oh, that's priceless. You can keep this one, Ben, if you like.'

'I do like,' Ben whispered in her ear as he slipped a possessive arm around her waist and steered her towards the house.

But, even as she quivered inside with delicious pleasure at his touch, Jess knew Ben had no intention of keeping her. They would be together whilst he was here. And then he would go back to America and it would all be over.

CHAPTER NINE

ANDY'S PARENTS WERE as lovely as their home. Jess had been half-expecting that they would be snobbish, since they were wealthy and owned a winery. But they were anything but. Whilst obviously well-educated and well-spoken, both of them were very down to earth and welcoming, insisting immediately upon introduction that she call them Glen and Heather.

Afternoon tea had been set up in the main living room which had French doors leading out onto the veranda. Heather explained that it was a little too breezy today to have it out there, a wind having sprung up seemingly out of nowhere.

Jess had just finished her cup of tea and was popping a second delicious mini muffin into her mouth when a nearby phone rang. Not the ring tone of a mobile. The unmistakable sound of a landline.

'Do excuse me,' Heather said, moving over to a long sofa table which rested against the wall and on which sat a phone, along with some very nice pieces of pottery.

Jess tried not to listen but it was impossible once she heard Heather make a sound which was halfway between a gasp and a groan.

'Oh, my dear, that's most unfortunate,' she said to whoever she was talking to. 'So what are you going to do? Yes, yes, I'll get Andy for you right away.'

Andy's attention must already have been grabbed because he jumped up immediately and rushed to take the phone from his mother. It didn't take Einstein to realise he was talking to his fiancée and that something had gone wrong. Heather, thank God, quickly enlightened the rest of them.

'Catherine's matron of honour has been rushed to hospital with a threatened miscarriage. Anyway, she's okay, but she has to stay in bed for at least a week and can't be at the wedding tomorrow. She's naturally very upset. Catherine is too. I suppose she'll just have to move the other bridesmaid up to be opposite you, Ben. It means it will be a very small bridal party, but what else can she do?'

Murphy's Law had struck, was Jess's immediate thought. And cruelly. She felt terribly sorry for them all, but especially the bride.

'She could always put Jess in her place,' Ben suddenly suggested.

Jess threw him a horrified look. 'Don't be ridiculous, Ben. Andy's fiancée doesn't even *know* me.'

'In that case, we'll take you over to her place and she can meet you,' he said in his usual taking over fashion. 'She only lives next door. It's not an ideal solution, Heather,' he said, turning his attention to Andy's mother, 'but it *is* a solution.'

'Well, yes, I...I suppose so,' Heather said before Jess could object again. 'It would also make Krissie feel better. She thinks she's spoiled her best friend's wedding. Not to mention the wedding photos. Catherine was only having the two bridesmaids and now she's down to one.'

'It's a perfectly sensible solution,' Glen said with typical male pragmatism. 'Andy!' he called out. 'Ben here said Jess would be willing to take Krissie's place, if it's all right with Catherine.'

Jess held her breath whilst Andy explained Ben's suggestion to his bride.

'She's Ben's new girlfriend,' Andy went on when he was obviously asked for further explanation. 'Her name is Jess. They only met recently. Over some business deal in Sydney. Anyway, Ben got his rental car totalled by some drunk and Jess offered to drive him out here... She'll look great in the wedding photos.'

Jess cringed, not sure now if she wanted the bride to say yay or nay. Still, it wasn't as though she wouldn't have been at the wedding anyway. And if it made everyone a bit happier... After all, weddings were supposed to be happy occasions.

Andy turned to face Jess. 'She says thanks heaps for the offer. Says you've really saved the day, but she would still have to see you asap. Something about whether the dress would fit you or not. It might need altering. Krissie was pregnant, after all.'

'Fine,' Ben said, standing up. 'Tell Catherine we'll be over straight away.'

After Andy relayed Ben's message, he shot his friend a droll look. 'She says *I'm* not allowed to come. Something about my not being allowed to see any of the dresses before the big day.' He rolled his eyes and placed his hand over the phone. 'Women! *Truly.*'

'No sweat, Andy. Tell Catherine we're on our way.' Taking Jess's hand, Ben pulled her to her feet, made his excuses to an understanding Glen and Heather, then steered Jess from the room.

'Make sure you're back for tonight, Ben,' Andy threw after them.

'Will do,' Ben threw back.

Jess resisted resorting to belated objections on the way out. What was done was done.

'Don't be angry with me,' Ben said as they climbed into their respective seats in the SUV.

'I'm not,' Jess said with a somewhat resigned sigh, then started the engine. 'But it might be an idea if you didn't always presume I would do whatever you wanted. A girl likes to be consulted first.'

He seemed startled by her stand. Clearly, he was used to women kow-towing to him all the time.

'Sorry,' he said. 'I was just trying to fix things for Andy.'

'Yes, I know that. That's why I'm not angry.'

'Good. But I will try to be more thoughtful in future. Right, you just turn left when we hit the main road and it's the next driveway along. Catherine's parents own a horse stud. Racehorses.'

'So they're rich too?'

'Not as rich as Andy's folks. But, yes, they're well off.'

'Do you have any poor friends?'

Ben hesitated before answering.

'Not many,' he said.

'I thought not,' she said drily. Rich people mixed with rich people. She was the odd one out here.

'There's the driveway,' he said, pointing.

This one was more impressive than Andy's driveway, with a huge, black iron archway connecting the tall brick gateposts with the name 'Winning Post Stud' outlined in red. The road itself—which was concreted rather than tarred—was lined with white-painted wooden fences behind which grazed the most beautiful horses Jess had ever seen, some of them with foals at foot. She wasn't a horse person herself but her father liked a flutter on the races and she always had a bet on the Melbourne Cup every year. Often won too, which piqued her dad considerably, since she knew next to nothing about form. Mostly she just picked names that she liked.

The house itself was similar in style to Heather and Glen's but genuinely old, made of stone rather than wood. It was also two-storeyed with iron lacework on the verandas and lots of chimneys.

Jess parked outside the large shed behind the house.

'Before we go in, exactly what did you tell Andy about me?'

'I said you were a marketing consultant I'd met connected with Fab Fashions. But I did let him think we'd met a week or so back, not this morning.'

His reminding her that they'd just met today startled Jess. It underlined just how far they'd come in a few short hours. She should have been more shocked, she supposed. But she was beyond shock. When she shook her head in a type of confusion, he leant over and brushed his lips over hers.

'Don't stress the small stuff, Jess,' he murmured against her quivering mouth. 'Just go with the flow.'

When his head lifted she blinked up at him. He wasn't a flow, she realised. He was a raging current which threatened to carry her out to sea and leave her there, like so much flotsam.

'Ah, here's Catherine, and presumably the other bridesmaid, come to meet us,' Ben said and reached for the door handle.

With an effort, Jess pulled herself together.

Catherine turned out to be a right sweetie. Late twenties, Jess guessed. Above-average height, with an athletic figure and blonde hair. Possibly not a natural blonde, but it suited her. She was very attractive with blue eyes and a warm, friendly manner. Nothing bitchy or snobby about her at all. Jess didn't like her bridesmaid nearly as much, perhaps because she made eyes at Ben from the moment she made an appearance. Her name was Leanne and she and Catherine had gone to boarding school together at some college in Bathurst, along with Krissie, who was the only one of the three friends who'd married so far.

'The teachers at school called us "the unholy trinity",' Catherine said, smiling.

'We *were* a bit naughty,' Leanne trilled.

'I can't believe that,' Ben said, annoying Jess with his flirtatious tone. If he was trying to make her jealous, then he was being successful!

After a little more idle chit-chat, Jess and Ben were led inside the house, where they refused offers of another afternoon tea from Catherine's harried-looking mother. Her name was Joan, a handsome woman, but way too thin, with anxious eyes.

'We just had afternoon tea at Andy's place,' Ben explained.

'I see,' she muttered, then gave Jess a frowning once-over. 'You're a lovely looking girl, dear, but I don't think you're going to fit into Krissie's dress.'

'I don't think so either,' Catherine agreed. 'Luckily, she's about the same height as Krissie, but I'd say she's a good size smaller. Krissie's put on some weight since getting pregnant. But no worries, Mum. At least she's not too big. There's nothing Doris could do to make the dress bigger, but making it smaller is not so much of a problem.

'Doris is a lady in Mudgee who does alterations for Mum and me,' she explained to Ben and Jess. 'I'll give her a call once I know what needs to be done. Meanwhile, we should go upstairs and try the dress on post haste. Then I'll ring her. No, no, you stay down here, Ben,' Catherine added when he went to follow them. 'You're not allowed to see the dresses either. You might tell Andy about them and that's bad luck. Mum, take Ben into the living room and put the TV on.'

It rather amused Jess to see the look on Ben's face. Clearly, he wasn't used to being told what to do, especially by women. Most of them probably said yes to him all the time. Jess realised it would do Ben good if she rejected him tomorrow night. But she couldn't see that happening. She would kick herself if she let him go back to America without spending at least one night with him.

Not knowing what it would have been like would haunt her for ever!

'Don't worry,' Catherine said in a conspiratorial whisper as she led Jess up a large, curving staircase, a reluctant Leanne in their wake. 'He won't go anywhere whilst we're gone.'

Jess laughed. 'Well, he can't, can he? He can't drive.'

'Gosh, that must be hard for him. I know Andy would die if he couldn't drive. Is Ben badly hurt?'

'Only his ego,' Jess replied.

'He's very sweet,' Leanne defended from behind them. 'And very rich.'

'Is he?' Jess said casually.

'You said his dad was a billionaire, didn't you, Catherine?'

'That's what Andy told me,' Catherine confirmed.

Jess shrugged. 'Well, that's his dad, not him.'

'But he's an only child,' Leanne persisted as Catherine led Jess into her bedroom, which was huge.

'I'm not interested in Ben for his money,' she said a bit sharply.

'Are you serious about each other?' Catherine asked.

'We've only just met, but we like each other a lot I think...' Jess replied. She didn't want anyone thinking she was that easy. *She* didn't like thinking she was going to be that easy.

Catherine smiled over her shoulder. 'Well, let's get this dress on and see what has to be done.'

The dress was pale-pink chiffon lined with satin, strapless in style with a seam straight under the bust from which the skirt fell in feminine folds to the floor. It was a sweet dress—not Jess's usual style, but surprisingly it looked good on her, the pale pink suiting her strong colouring. It was not a colour she ever chose for herself, thinking she needed bolder colours.

The dress was too large in the bust line, however. The bodice was just too wide. It needed to be taken in at the side seams which would be a time-consuming job; both the chiffon and the lining would have to be carefully unpicked before being resewn. Thankfully, it was the right length, Krissie obviously being of a similar height to Jess. And, whilst the matching shoes were half a size too large, it was better than them being too small.

Catherine tipped her head to one side as she looked Jess over. 'It actually looks better on you than it did on Krissie. But I won't be telling her that,' she added with a quick smile. 'She feels bad enough as it is. Anyway, I'll just give Doris a call. She altered my wedding dress for me a couple of weeks ago when I lost weight. I'm sure she won't mind, since it's an emergency.'

But as it turned out Doris was in Melbourne visiting her sister.

Murphy's Law at work again, Jess thought silently as she took off the dress and put her own clothes back on again. But at least she could do something about the dismay which had already entered the bride-to-be's face.

'It'll be all right, Catherine,' she said soothingly. 'I can fix the dress. I know exactly what to do. And, before you ask, I have my trusty sewing machine sitting in the back of my four-wheel drive.'

Both Catherine and Leanne gaped at her.

'But...but...' Catherine stammered, not looking too certain about Jess's offer.

Jess smiled reassuringly. 'You don't have to worry. I'm a very experienced dressmaker. It was my profession before I went into marketing,' she added, backing up Ben's little white lie. 'I made this jacket myself, you know, and I think it's a pretty good design.'

'You can say that again!' Catherine exclaimed. 'I've been envying it ever since you arrived.'

'Me too,' Leanne gushed. 'Floral jackets are very *in* this spring.'

'But tell me something, Jess,' Catherine said, looking puzzled. 'Do you *always* travel around with your sewing machine?'

Jess realised immediately she could hardly say that, until fate had stepped in and changed everything, she'd been going to do some sewing whilst she was stuck in a motel room for most of the weekend.

'Lord, no,' she said, laughing. 'I simply forgot to take it out of the car after I did some sewing at a girlfriend's place last weekend. How lucky is that?' As little white lies went, it wasn't too bad, except that it made Jess realise she didn't have girlfriends the way Catherine did. When she'd left Sydney to come live on the Central Coast she'd drifted away from all the female friends she'd made at school. She did see a couple of them occasionally but they weren't in her life on a regular basis. In truth, she didn't actually have any female friends now that Colin had debunked, her recent social life having been more his mates and *their* girlfriends.

Jess had never thought of herself as being lonely before. She did have a large family, but suddenly she envied Catherine her girlfriends.

Still, she didn't entertain her negative feelings for long, vowing instead to do something about her lack of girlfriends once she got back home. Maybe she would join a gym. Or a sports club of some kind. She'd been good at basketball at school, her above-average height giving her an advantage. Yes, she'd join a basketball club. For females only. Jess suspected that after Ben went back to America she would want a spell away from male company for a while.

Her heart lurched at this last thought but she steadfastly ignored it.

'How about I drive Ben back to Andy's place?' she suggested. 'Then come back and get stuck into the dress? It could take a couple of hours. I don't want to rush things. I want to get it right.'

Catherine beamed at her. 'Jess, you are a life saver! You must stay here for dinner,' Catherine added. 'Then afterwards we can have a little hen party of our own. I mean, there's no point in your returning to Andy's place. He and Ben are going out on the town in Mudgee tonight. A few of their mates from uni are staying at a motel there, so they're having a big get-together. I did tell Andy not to stay out too late or do anything seriously stupid, but you know Aussie men when they get a few beers into them. Ben might sound like an American these days, but he's an Aussie boy through and through.'

Jess didn't agree with Catherine on that score. Ben was nothing like any Aussie boy she'd ever met.

'At least the wedding's not till four-thirty,' Catherine added. 'So they have time to recover.'

'Where is the wedding, Catherine?' Jess asked.

'We're having it outside in Mum's rose garden, with a

celebrant officiating. And the reception will be in a marquee set up on the back lawn. It's due to go up first thing in the morning. Once that's done, the wedding planner and her lot will swoop in and set everything else up.'

'You booked a wedding planner?' Jess said, surprised. She would want to plan her own wedding right down to the last detail.

'Gosh, yes. I knew it would be a nightmare if I did it. Mum would want to help, but the poor love gets in a flap over the least little thing. The lady I hired has been fantastic. She's arranged everything, right down to the cars and the flowers. She even took me down to Sydney and helped me choose the dresses. Not that it's a large wedding. Only about a hundred guests. This business with Krissie and her dress is the first hiccup there's been.'

'Is the weather forecast good for tomorrow?' Jess asked, worried that Murphy's Law might raise its ugly head again at the last minute. She was beginning to be a serious believer.

'Perfect. Warm, with no rain in sight. Okay, let's get ourselves downstairs and I'll reassure Mum whilst you drop Ben back at Andy's. But don't be away too long,' she added, flashing Jess a knowing smile. 'No hanky panky, now. Keep that till after the wedding.'

CHAPTER TEN

'ARE YOU SURE you can do this, Jess?' Ben said as Jess sped down the driveway. 'I mean, altering a dress can't be the same as making one from scratch.'

'It won't be any trouble. Gran did a lot of alterations and I used to help her. I earned my first pocket money that way.'

'You are full of surprises, aren't you?' he said, smiling over at her. 'A good person to have around, I would imagine. I dare say you can cook as well.'

Jess shrugged. 'I'm not bad. Mum's better, though. Can you cook? Or is that a silly question?'

'Not at all. I think all men should be able to cook a bit, especially ones who live alone. I can make a mean omelette, and my mushroom risotto has received several compliments.'

Jess laughed. 'I dare say it has.' She could imagine Amber gushing over every single thing he did. She could hear her now: *Oh, Ben, darling, you are so clever. And talented. And handsome. And rich.*

No, no, Amber wouldn't actually say that last bit. She would not be as obvious as Leanne. Or as envious. Because Amber would have money of her own. Jess was sure of it.

His sideways glance was sharp. 'Do I detect some sarcasm in that remark?'

Her returning glance was brilliantly po-faced. Or so she thought.

'Not at all.'

He chuckled. 'You little liar, you. You enjoy taking the Mickey out of me.'

'That's a very Aussie saying. Maybe you're not as American as you sound.'

'What's wrong with being American?'

'Absolutely nothing.' It was his being a *filthy rich* American that was the problem.

'You're not going to sleep the night at Catherine's place, are you?' he asked abruptly.

Jess frowned at this question. 'I wasn't planning to, but what difference would it make if I did? You're going out and from what I gather you'll be home very late.'

'I just want you to be there in the morning. I want to have breakfast with you and talk to you some more.'

'Okay,' she agreed. 'But do try to be quiet when you get in. I'm going to be tired after doing that dress. I don't want to be woken by drunken revellers.'

'I have no intention of getting drunk tonight,' he surprised her by saying. 'I don't want to be hung-over tomorrow, thank you very much. I have plans for tomorrow night which require me to be fit and well.'

'Oh,' she said, and for the first time in her life Jess blushed. But it wasn't the blush of embarrassment, it was the blush of heat. Sexual heat.

'Don't miss Andy's place,' he said.

'What? Oh, God, I forgot where I was for a moment.' She glanced in the rear-view mirror as she braked sharply before turning into Andy's driveway.

'Thinking of tomorrow night?' he asked in a low, oh, so sexy voice.

Jess refused to act rattled by him, even though she was.

'But of course,' she said, her cool tone a total contrast to the inferno raging inside her.

Ben should not have been surprised by her bald honesty. Jess didn't play games. But Ben had games very much in mind for tomorrow night. He didn't want sex with her to be over quickly. He wanted to savour it. To savour her. He also wanted the love-making to last and last and last.

'How many lovers have you had, Jess?'

'Not as many as you've had, I'll bet,' she countered, thinking he had a hide to ask her that. 'Now, could we stop talking about sex?' She reefed the car to a ragged halt. 'You sit here whilst I go get Andy, and I'll explain things, then find out where this guest cottage is. And, before you object, you're not fooling me by pretending you can get in and out of your seat without some pain in your shoulder because I know differently. So just be a good boy and sit still for a while.'

She didn't give him a chance to come back with some witty riposte because she was off in a flash, running up the side steps of the house, leaving Ben to ponder just how good a boy he was going to be tonight. And he wasn't talking about at the stag party.

The temptation to come home early was acute. He could easily make some excuse pertaining to his car accident— claim a crippling headache from the concussion, or an appallingly painful shoulder. It *was* sore, but nothing to write home about.

No, he decided in the end. He would wait. Waiting often made the sex better. And Jess would be even more inclined to be thoroughly seduced.

Tomorrow night would be a first for him in more ways than one. His first wedding. His first brunette. The first girl in a decade who didn't seem overly impressed with his being Morgan De Silva's son and heir.

Now, that really would be a first!

CHAPTER ELEVEN

THE GUEST COTTAGE was cute and quite a long way from the main house, set on a smaller hill and surrounded by trees. Made of weatherboard, it had a pitched iron roof, covered porches front and back and a hallway which cut the cottage in two. On the left on entering was a lounge followed by a dining room and then the kitchen. On the right were two bedrooms separated by a bathroom, followed by a utility room and walk-in pantry. All the rooms were delightfully furnished in comfy, country-style furniture which was probably newer than it looked. Apparently, it had once been a miner's cottage, and had been on the property when Andy's parents had bought the place.

Andy had shown them the way to the cottage personally, which was a relief to Jess. Nothing like a third person being present to prevent Ben doing something which she didn't want him to do. Not yet, anyway. If truth be told, she was terrified of that moment when he would stop the talk and walk the walk, so to speak. She'd always thought herself quite good at sex but, on a scale of one to ten, she doubted she came much above a five. She would hate it if he found her a disappointment.

She quickly put her overnight bag in the smaller of the two bedrooms, insisting that Ben have the front room with the queen-sized bed, since he was too big for a single bed.

He didn't argue, just sat down on the side of the bed and bounced up and down, as though testing it for comfort. Andy carried Ben's things into the room whilst Jess hovered in the doorway.

'I'll come back with some more provisions shortly,' Andy told them. 'Some stuff for breakfast. There's already white wine in the fridge, and red wine in the cupboards, along with coffee, tea and biscuits, etc. But I'll bring down some fresh bread, eggs and bacon.'

'Well, I won't be here,' Jess returned before he could escape. 'I have to get back to Catherine's. I won't be back till late tonight.'

'Oh, right. I forgot. I also forgot to thank you for what you're doing, Jess. Catherine rang me and told me about the dress. You are one clever girl, isn't she, Ben? Fancy being able to sew like that.'

'She's amazing,' Ben said.

Jess just smiled, awake to his many compliments.

The moment they were alone Ben gave her a narrow-eyed look. 'You won't be staying in that bedroom tomorrow night.'

She glowered at him, never being at her best when men started ordering her around. 'Maybe I will,' she bit out. 'If you start acting like some jerk.'

That sent him back in his heels. 'What do you mean?'

'I run my own race, Ben. I don't like men telling me what to do and when to do it.'

'Is that so?'

Ben stood up and strode over to her, taking her firmly by the shoulders and pulling her hard against him. She didn't struggle, or protest. Just stared up at him with wide, dilated eyes. Ben could actually feel her galloping heartbeat. She thought she didn't like to be ordered around, but he knew that a lot of strong-minded women liked their lovers to take charge.

It came to him that she'd probably never had a dominant lover before. What an exciting thought!

He could hardly wait for tomorrow night to come.

'When the time is right, Jess,' he said quietly, his eyes intense on hers, 'you *will* like me telling you what to do. Trust me on this. But, for now, perhaps you should get going. Because if you stay I won't be responsible for what might happen.'

Jess left the cottage in a fluster, her body cruelly turned on and her thoughts totally scattered.

Trust him, he'd said. To do what? Turn her into some kind of mindless sex slave?

At this moment she didn't doubt he could do it. If she let him.

Did she want that to happen?

The answer to that question lay in her thudding heart and rock-hard nipples.

Suddenly, Jess was overwhelmed by a wave of desire so strong that she almost ran off the road. Giving herself a savage mental shake, she slowed down to a crawl, then turned shakily into Catherine's driveway, proceeding very carefully up the cement road, grateful now that she had a job to do which would take her most of the evening; *very* grateful that she had no reason to go back to that seductive cottage till well after Ben had left with Andy for their night on the town. Thank heavens he wouldn't get home till the small hours of the morning. By which time she would be sound asleep.

Jess had to laugh over that one. There would be no sleeping for her tonight.

But at least she could pretend she was asleep.

Things didn't turn out quite like that, however. Jess finished the dress around nine-thirty, after which she refused all offers of wine, saying she was tired, then drove back to the cottage. In actual fact she'd only just remembered that she'd promised to give her mother a ring. This she did whilst she opened a bottle of the white wine resting in the door of the fridge. She poured herself a large glass, sipping it as she sat at the kitchen table, and gave her mother an edited version of what had happened, telling her the truth about the dramas over the wedding and how she'd fixed the dress tonight, plus the plan for her to be a substitute matron of honour the next day. Naturally, she didn't mention anything about her being thought of as Ben's girlfriend or that she was staying with him, alone, in this cottage. She admitted staying as a guest at the winery but that was all.

'It sounds like it's been a rather surprising trip so far,' her mother said.

'It certainly has,' Jess agreed with considerable irony as she poured herself a second glass of wine.

'You'll have to ring me tomorrow night and tell me all about the wedding.'

Jess winced. She could hardly tell her mother why that wasn't going to happen.

'Mum, the wedding's not till late in the afternoon. By the time the reception is over and I get to bed, it's going to be very late and I'm going to be exhausted. I'll call you on Sunday morning. But not too early, mind. I might sleep in.' Jess was grateful that her mother couldn't see inside her head at this moment, as the images in there were not fit for a caring mother's consumption.

'Oh, all right,' her mother said. 'But don't forget to take some photos. I'd love to see what you looked like. What you *all* looked like, actually. Which reminds me. What does this Ben fellow look like? You said he was nice but I have a feeling he's good-looking, am I right?'

'Yes, he's very good-looking,' she admitted, struggling to keep her voice calm in the face of a looming panic attack over her sexual inadequacies. 'And very tall.'

'Tall, dark and handsome, eh?'

'No, he's actually fair-haired, with blue eyes.'

'And how old, did you say?'

'I don't know. Early thirties, perhaps.'

'And rich?'

'Filthy rich, Mum. His father's a billionaire.'

'Goodness. And did you tell him that you lost your job at Fab Fashions because of him?'

'I did mention it. And he promised to see what he could do.'

'Well, that was nice of him. But did he mean it?'

The jury was still out on that score. 'Maybe. I guess we'll have to wait and see, Mum. Now, I really must go. I'm tired.' That was a lie. She had so much adrenaline flowing through her body at the moment that she had no hope of sleeping. That was why she was downing all this wine; sometimes wine made her sleepy. Unfortunately, it didn't seem to be working.

'Driving can be very tiring,' her mother said. 'Goodnight, darling. Sleep tight. Love you.'

Jess suddenly came over all emotional.

'Love you too, Mum,' she choked out, then hung up.

Jess decided after her third glass of wine that it definitely wasn't working. So she put the half-drunk bottle back in the fridge and headed for the bathroom. A long, hot bath filled in another hour but didn't relax her one iota. She'd just emerged from the bathroom, dressed in a nightie, when she heard a car screech to a stop in front of the cottage. Running to the front living room, Jess peered through the curtains in time to see Ben climb out of the back of a taxi.

Flustered—what on earth was he doing home this early?—she whirled to make a dash for the bedroom, in her haste catching her left foot under the curled up corner of a rug. She cried out as she fell, her hands bracing themselves to protect her face whilst her knees hit the wooden floorboards with a painful thud.

Ben heard Jess cry out as he made his way up onto the front veranda. He dashed inside, switching on the hall light and calling her name at the same time.

He found her sitting back on her haunches in the semidark on the living-room floor, dressed in a red satin nightie with spaghetti straps which showed off her gorgeous figure. Her lovely hair was down, spread over her shoulders in dishevelled disarray, adding to the criminally sexy picture she presented.

'What happened?' he asked, and held out his left hand to help her up.

'I fell over,' she said, but made no move to take his hand, her eyes on her ground. 'My foot got caught under the rug.'

'I see,' he said, not seeing at all. What was she doing in this room, anyway? The lights weren't on. Neither was the television. 'Well, do you want to take my hand or are you going to stay there all night?' he said, his tone betraying his inner frustration.

She glanced up at him.

Jess only just managed not to groan out loud. God, but he looked utterly gorgeous dressed in grey stone-washed jeans, an open-necked white shirt and a fabulous looking charcoal-grey jacket.

Finally, she placed her hand in his, his fingers closing tightly around hers as he pulled her to her feet.

'What on earth are you doing home *this* early?' she asked whilst she tried to ignore the direction of his gaze. Right where her erect nipples were poking against the red satin. Maybe he would think she was cold. Though she wasn't, having turned off the air-conditioning when she'd got home. The temperature had dropped considerably once the sun had gone down but it was a nice twenty-three degrees inside the cottage.

'Do you want the truth?'

'Of course.'

'I told Andy I had a vicious headache and that if he wanted me on deck tomorrow, then I should go home.'

'And do you? Have a vicious headache?'

'No. I simply couldn't stop thinking about you.'

Jess tried not to let his flattering words seduce her but it was way too late for such a futile struggle.

'I've been thinking about you too,' she admitted somewhat shakily.

'So do I still have to wait till tomorrow night?'

She shook her head.

She half-expected him to kiss her then but he didn't. Instead, he just smiled.

'I need a shower,' he said. 'I smell of beer. Can I tempt you to join me?'

The desire to lick her suddenly dry lips was intense but somehow she resisted. Jess swallowed instead, putting some moisture into her mouth. 'I…I've just had a bath,' she said, her voice thick and throaty.

'Then you can come and watch.'

Jess blinked at him, her mouth falling open briefly before snapping shut again.

'All right,' she said, wondering if this was what he'd meant earlier about her liking him telling her what to do.

She did. Which was weird. If Colin or any of her other boyfriends had suggested the same thing to her, she would have told them to get lost. Bathrooms were private places, in her opinion. They weren't places where you *watched*. Yet she wanted to watch Ben shower, didn't she? She wanted to see him naked. Wanted to do all sorts of things she'd never done before.

Her head spun at the thought.

When she didn't move, he frowned at her. 'You've changed your mind already?'

Changed her mind? Was he insane? How could she possibly change her mind when she'd already lost it?

She shook her head.

'Good,' he said, and held out his hand to her again.

CHAPTER TWELVE

BEN LIKED THE way Jess let him lead her meekly into the bathroom. He could tell she was turned on, the same way he was. Even the slightest touch turned him on with her. It was quite incredible, the effect she had on him. But nothing he couldn't control, now that she was being deliciously cooperative.

He settled her, somewhat stunned-looking, on the side of the claw-footed bath, then started undressing.

Jess could not believe she was doing this, sitting there watching whilst Ben took all his clothes off in front of her. But, dear heaven, it was exciting!

After he kicked off his shoes, he removed his jacket and then his shirt, revealing an upper half which didn't look like it spent all day seated behind a desk. He must work hard in a gym, she decided, or go swimming a lot. His light tan suggested this might be the case. He had broad shoulders, one of which carried a nasty bruise. But it didn't seem to stop his arm working. His chest muscles were wide and well-toned, his stomach a surprising six-pack. Very little body hair, she noted, and liked.

Jess held her breath when he whipped the belt out of his jeans, but he just dropped it on the floor, then ran the zipper down. When his hands hooked under the waist band

and pushed down, she finally let go of the air trapped in her lungs.

He was wearing black underpants, made out of a silky material which hid nothing.

She wondered if he was as big as he looked. Jess had always believed that size *did* matter. To a degree. She liked a man to be well built in that area.

He was. Bigger than her previous boyfriends. And magnificently erect. Circumcised, with only a smattering of fair hair at the base. She knew he would feel—and taste— fantastic.

He stood facing her, a golden Adonis in every way.

'Now you, Jess,' he commanded. 'Stand up and take that nightie off. I want to see all of you.'

She stood up onto shaky legs, utterly compelled to obey him. Her belly tightened as she slowly slipped the straps off her shoulders, first on, then the other. She wasn't wearing any undies. She never wore undies to bed. The nightie slid down her body with a whoosh, pooling around her feet on the tiled floor.

His gaze dropped down to those feet first, then gradually travelled upwards, lingering on the neatly waxed V of curls between her thighs, before lifting to her breasts.

'Beautiful,' he said.

Jess knew she was attractive, but she'd never considered herself beautiful. She had physical flaws, like most people. Couldn't Ben see that her nose was too big for her face? So was her mouth. The back of her thighs had some dimples of cellulite which no amount of massage or cream could remove, though he wouldn't see that unless he ordered her to turn around.

Jess suspected Ben wasn't about to do that. He was enjoying looking at her breasts too much. Admittedly, they were the best feature of her figure. Full and high, with perky pink nipples that grew astonishingly in size when they were played with. Or when she was excited. Which she was right now. God, yes. Her whole breasts seemed to be swelling under his hot, hungry eyes, though perhaps it was just Jess's ragged breathing.

'No more arguments or excuses, Jess,' he said thickly. 'You're coming into that shower with me and then we're going to bed. Together.'

Once again, she obeyed him, blindly and without protest, letting him pull her with him into the shower cubicle. And it was there, as the hot jets of waters did dreadful things to her hair, that he cupped her face and finally kissed her properly.

Jess had been kissed many times in her life. And by men who were quite good kissers. But Ben kissing her was a once-in-a-lifetime experience. She felt its effect through her whole body right down to her toes. It overwhelmed her. Then obsessed her. She could not get enough of it. And of him. When at last his head lifted, she sank against him in total surrender, her arms wrapping tightly around his waist.

'Are you on the pill, Jess?'

She pulled back enough to glance up at him. 'What?'

'Are you on the pill?'

Her mind cleared a little. 'Well…yes…but…'

'You still want me to use protection.'

'Please,' she said, despite being tempted to say no. *Just do it to me. Right here and now.*

'In that case, I think we should cut this shower short this time.'

Again, no protest from her. She just stood there whilst he switched off the taps, then reached for one of the towels hanging on the rack, rubbing rather roughly at her dripping hair before giving himself a brisk rub down. Then he scooped her up in his arms and carried her back to his bedroom.

Jess shivered as he laid her gently down on top of the bed, goose bumps springing up over her body.

'Are you cold?' he asked as he lay down next to her, propping himself up on his left side.

'A little,' she lied.

'Do you want to get under the covers?'

She shook her head.

'I've been wanting to do this all day,' he said, and bent his lips to hers once more, his right hand sliding up into her still damp hair.

His return to gentle kisses surprised her at first, then entranced her. She sighed under their soft sweetness. Gradually, however, the pressure of his mouth grew stronger. When his teeth nipped at her lower lip, she gasped, and his tongue slipped inside once more, Jess moaning softly as it explored the sensitive skin of her palate. She gasped again when a hand covered her right breast, playing with her nipple in ways she'd definitely never experienced before: soft rubbing with his palm interspersed with quite painful pinching till it was on fire.

And all the while he kept on kissing her, his tongue alternately snaking deep, then withdrawing before plunging in again. When his hand moved across to her other nipple, she felt momentarily bereft for the abandoned one. If he could have played with both at the same time, she would have been in heaven. Or hell. Jess could not work out if she was in agony or ecstasy. Not that she cared, as long as he didn't stop.

He stopped, both the kissing and the nipple pinching, leaving her moaning in dismay till she realised why he'd stopped. Already he was down there with that knowing mouth and tongue of his, making her groan and squirm as he licked and sucked and showed her that all her other lovers had been seriously ignorant of a woman's body. Ben knew exactly what to do to bring her to the brink of coming, not once but several times. How he knew when to back off, she wasn't sure. Maybe it had something to do with his fingers being deep inside her all the while. Maybe he could feel the way her muscles tightened when she came close to coming.

His head lifted at last. 'Enough, I think,' he muttered, then collapsed on his back beside her, breathing very heavily.

She levered herself up onto her elbow and stared over at him. 'You're not stopping, are you?'

'Just for a few seconds. I need a breather, and then I have to get a condom on. I put two in that top drawer this afternoon,' he said, nodding towards the bedside chest next to her. 'Get one for me, would you, Jess?'

Jess wondered if Ben always used protection, even when his girlfriends were on the pill. She had a feeling that he did. Maybe he was worried that one of them might try to trap him into marriage. Seriously rich men would have to worry about such things, she imagined. If this Amber wanted to marry him enough, it wouldn't be beyond her to do such thing.

'Put it on for me,' he said after she extracted one from the drawer.

Oh, Lord, Jess thought as she opened the foil packet and turned back to him. She *had* put a condom on before. Just not whilst she was in such an excited state. She found it extremely difficult with her hands shaking so much. When Ben groaned, she shot him a worried look.

'Am I hurting you?'

His smile was both tortured and wry. 'Oh, honey, you're killing me. But not in the way you think. Would you mind being on top?'

'You want me on top?' she echoed. Whilst it was her favourite position, she hadn't imagined it would be Ben's. Earlier on, he'd seemed keen to be the one in control. And whilst it had turned her on, being ordered around, she was happy to have their roles reversed for a while. Though the position had been *his* idea, come to think of it.

'I would have thought you'd like being on top,' he said.

'I do quite like it,' she confessed.

'Then what are you waiting for?'

What, indeed?

Ben's stomach tightened when she moved to straddle him, his heart thundering in his chest when she took hold of him and presented the bursting tip against the entrance to her body. He could feel the heat and the wetness of her, but he couldn't see it. She wasn't one of those girls who totally denuded herself of body hair, her sex protected by a smattering of soft dark curls. Ben rather liked that. It was different. She was different. In every way. There was no pretence about her. She was sweet and very natural, and he wanted her as he'd never wanted any woman before. His excitement was so great that he had no patience with playing games tonight. He wanted her now!

A groan escaped his lips as she pushed him inside, her flesh slowly swallowing his with a silky snugness which was incredibly pleasurable. He braced himself mentally against what it would feel like when she moved. He didn't want to come too soon. Hell, no. That would never do!

Jess had been right. It felt incredible with him deep inside her, filling her totally. He obviously liked it too, judging by the look on his face. Though was it rapture she was seeing, or torture? A mixture of both, she imagined. Men could be very impatient at this stage. So she kept her movements slow and gentle at first, lifting her hips only slightly before lowering herself down again. But it wasn't long before her own desire for satisfaction took over, urging her to lift her hips higher, then to plunge down harder. She tried not to think about anything but her sexual pleasure, valiantly ignoring the emotional responses which hovered at the edges of her brain. This wasn't love, she told herself firmly. This was just sex. Great sex, yes, with an utterly gorgeous man. But still just sex. *Enjoy it, girl. Because you could go the rest of your life without finding a lover like Ben.*

Their coming together distracted her totally from any thought of love, her own orgasm so intense that all she could think about were the physical sensations. The electric pleasure of each spasm, plus the wonderful relief from the tension which had gripped her all evening. Finally, when it was over, every pore in her body succumbed to a huge wave of languor. She collapsed across him, totally spent, sighing a long, sated sigh when he wrapped his arms around her, his lips in her hair.

'That was fantastic,' he whispered. '*You're* fantastic.

'No, don't move,' he said when she tried to lift her head. 'I want to fall asleep like this, with me still inside you. My only regret is that we can't do it again. I'm just too damned tired all of a sudden. But I'll make it up to you tomorrow. I promise. Just stay where you are, you delicious thing. Stay,' he repeated, his voice slurring a little.

Within thirty seconds, he'd fallen asleep.

Less than a minute later, she followed him.

CHAPTER THIRTEEN

BEN WOKE TO the smell of bacon cooking, plus no Jess in bed with him. Hell, he'd really passed out last night. And slept for a good ten hours, he realised with amazement as he glanced at his watch. And whilst he regretted not waking—he hadn't intended sex with Jess to be so short and swift—the long sleep had done him a lot of good. His shoulder was one hundred percent better and he felt marvellous.

Ben fairly leapt out of bed, calling a hurried, 'Good morning,' out to Jess before bolting for the bathroom. After a very quick shower, he wrapped a towel around his waist, then made his way to the kitchen, anxious to see Jess again. She glanced over her shoulder as he walked in, her lovely eyes lighting up at the sight of him.

'You look good in a towel,' she said, smiling.

'And you look good in anything,' he returned, his gaze raking over her from top to toe. She was wearing the same fitted black trousers again, but her top was different, a simple scoop-necked sweater in a bright-green colour which suited her dark hair and olive skin. She wasn't wearing any make-up and her hair was up, secured on top of her head in a rather haphazard fashion. On closer inspection, he could see she'd wrapped it around itself in a knot, a few bits and pieces already escaping. Her lack of artifice continued to enchant him. Amber was always fully made up and her hair groomed to perfection before showing herself in the morning.

Jess made Amber look terribly shallow. And impossibly vain.

'Flatterer,' she said, laughing, then turned back to the stove.

'That smells good,' he said, coming up behind her to slide his arms around her waist.

Jess tried not to stiffen at his touch, having determined to act naturally with him. It had been difficult not to ogle his beautiful body when he'd come into the kitchen just now, but she'd managed, telling herself all the while that a sophisticated New York woman wouldn't ogle. She would sail through the morning after the night before with style and panache. She wouldn't ask for reassurances that he wanted more from her than sex. She would be pleasant and easy going. Slightly flirtatious, yes, but nothing heavy.

So, when Ben placed a hand under her chin and turned her face towards his, she hid her momentary panic and let him kiss her. Fortunately, it wasn't too deep, too long a kiss. But, oh…how her heart raced, her head instantly filling with images of him scattering everything off the kitchen table with one sweep of his arm and taking her on it then and there.

His eyes were glittering when his head lifted. 'If that bacon wasn't already cooked,' he said, 'I'd have *you* for breakfast.'

'Really,' she replied with superb nonchalance. 'I might have something to say about that.'

His eyes carried the knowledge she was bluffing. 'Come now, Jess, let's not play games this morning. You and I both know that what we shared last night was something special. And highly addictive. But you're right. We should eat first.'

'Your bruise looks much better,' she said, turning her attention back to the breakfast. 'When bruises start going all the colours of the rainbow, it usually means they're on the mend. Now, sit down, for Pete's sake, and let me get on with this.'

'You sound like you're familiar with bruises,' he said, pulling out a chair at the kitchen table and sitting down.

'I have three brothers,' she reminded him. 'There wasn't a day that they didn't come home from school with bruises.'

'Habitual fighters, were they?'

'No. Just physical.'

'Like you. You're very physical. And very sexy.'

Jess felt some dismay—and irritation—that Ben's focus seemed to be all about sex. She was more than that... wasn't she?

Somehow, she managed to serve up toast, bacon and eggs without burning anything. Ben ate his with relish, Jess just picking at hers. She'd always been a girl who lacked appetite when she was upset about something. She tried telling herself she was foolish to expect anything more than sex from Ben, but it was a losing cause.

'You didn't eat much,' Ben remarked after he finished his breakfast.

'I'm not very hungry. I had some coffee before you got up.'

'You're not one of those girls who lives on coffee, are you?'

'Not usually.'

'You don't need to lose weight, Jess. Your body is absolutely gorgeous just the way it is.'

Jess struggled not to show her feelings on her face. But did he *have* to concentrate on her body?

'I'm glad you think so. By the way, you said yesterday we could have a talk about Fab Fashions this morning.'

He seemed genuinely taken aback. 'Yes, I know I did. But that was before last night.'

Jess glared at him across the table. 'You mean you don't have to pander to me any more because we've already had sex.'

Ben hid his guilt well. Because she was right, wasn't she? But, damn it all, he wasn't about to waste time talking about business when he could be having sex with her again.

'No,' he said carefully. 'That's not true. Though what we shared last night does change things, Jess. It was so very special. We can talk about Fab Fashions during the drive home tomorrow. And every day next week. Meanwhile, we probably only have a couple of hours to ourselves before we both have to get ready for the wedding this afternoon. What time do you have to be over at Catherine's?'

She seemed mollified by his explanation. 'I said I'd be there at three. But I have to do my hair first. Catherine and Leanne are having their hair done at a hairdresser's in Mudgee this morning, but I prefer to do my own hair. I'm better at it than the hairdresser.'

He smiled. 'I have no doubt you are. Okay, Andy said he's going to collect me around two-thirty. We're all getting ready together up at the house before heading over to Catherine's around four. Apparently, it doesn't do for the groom's party to be late arriving.'

'You haven't been in a bridal party before?'

'Actually, no, I haven't. Have you?'

'I was a bridesmaid at all of my three brothers' weddings.'

'Maybe next time you'll be the bride.'

'I doubt it,' she said, her voice sharp.

'Don't you want to get married?'

'Well, yes, I do. Eventually. That's what we do in our

family. But I'm prepared to wait till the right man comes along. After Colin, I'm not in any hurry.'

Ben wasn't in any hurry either. But it did cross his mind that Jess would make some man a wonderful wife.

'And what would make him the right man?' he asked.

Jess shrugged. 'That's a difficult question. For starters, he'd have to be reasonably successful in whatever he's chosen to do in life. I like men who are confident.'

'Would he have to be rich?'

'Not rich like you, Ben De Silva. I would never marry a man as rich as you.'

Ben felt perversely offended. 'Really? A lot of women would.'

'Yeah. Silly, greedy ones like Leanne. And already rich ones like your Amber.'

Ben frowned. 'Why makes you think Amber's rich?'

Jess stood up and started clearing the breakfast things away. 'Am I wrong?' she threw at him.

'No. She *is* rich. Or, her father is.'

'I thought as much.'

Ben laughed. 'You're not jealous, are you, Jess? You have no reason to be. Amber's history.'

His accusing her of jealousy was very telling. Because she was. Horribly so. Jess turned her back on him and walked over to the sink. She'd be history too one day soon. It was just a matter of time. And geography.

His suddenly taking firm possession of her shoulders startled her. She hadn't even heard him get up.

'Don't be angry with me, Jess. Come back to bed. We can talk about Fab Fashions there, if you like. We can multi-task.'

She couldn't help it. She laughed. 'Men can't multi-task.'

'Don't you believe it,' he said as he pulled her back hard

against him. 'I can talk and get an erection at the same time. See?' he said and rubbed himself against her bottom. 'There's proof.'

She laughed some more.

'I love it when you laugh,' he murmured as he nuzzled her neck. 'But I love it more when you come. The sounds you make, the way your insides squeeze me like a vice... You drove me crazy last night. Drive me crazy again, lovely Jess. With your mouth this time. And those hands you're so damned good with.'

She was the one who was being driven crazy. No man had ever said things like that to her. He made her want to do *everything* with him. Oh, God...

She didn't say a word, just whirled in his arms and kissed him. And he kissed her back, a long, wet wildly passionate kiss which scattered her brainwaves and turned her body to liquid.

'Come on. Back to bed,' he said when he finally came up for air.

'Bed?' she echoed, dazed.

His smile was wry. 'Yeah. You know. The furniture thingy with sheets and pillows where you go to sleep at night. But we're not going to sleep in it today, beautiful,' he added. 'Not even for a single second.'

CHAPTER FOURTEEN

'DO YOU THINK I'm doing the right thing?'

Jess almost shook her head at the bride in exasperation. After all, why ask *her*? She knew next to nothing
of Catherine's relationship with Andy. It was also rather
late to have second thoughts with the bridal party about
to make its way over to the rose garden where the groom
would be impatiently waiting. They were already twenty
minutes behind schedule. At the same time, Jess did feel
some sympathy for the girl. Her mother was not the most
reassuring of mothers—the woman had spent the last two
hours in tears—and marriage *was* a big step, especially in
this day and age when divorce was rife and the 'for ever'
kind of love seemed like a pipe dream. But, as they said
in the classics, better to have loved and lost than never to
have loved at all!

'Do you love Andy, Catherine?' Jess asked quickly.

'Yes, of course.'

'There is no *of course* about it. Lots of girls marry for
reasons other than love.'

'Not me.'

'Nor me. And does Andy love you?'

'Yes, I'm sure he does.'

A sudden thought crossed Jess's mind. 'You're not pregnant, are you?'

'Lord, no. No. But we do plan on having children.'

'Sounds like you don't have any reason for last-minute doubts, Catherine. Now, come on, girl, we're already running late. Though, before you go, let me say you look absolutely gorgeous!' Which was true. Her dress was a bit OTT in Jess's opinion, but it suited Catherine's feminine blonde beauty.

'Oh.' The bride fairly beamed. 'You look gorgeous as well. And you too, Leanne.'

Leanne preened whilst Jess just smiled. Yes, they did all look very nice.

'Aren't you girls ready yet?' Catherine's father snarled at them.

Jess had disliked the man within seconds of having met him. He was one of those larger than life men who was absolutely full of himself. Jess decided with sudden insight that his bombast could explain why Catherine's mother was a nervous wreck and why perhaps Catherine was afraid of marriage. If Andy had been anything like her father in character—which fortunately he didn't seem to be—then she would have every right to be hesitant.

Jess decided to put him on the spot. 'Don't you think your daughter looks absolutely divine?'

'What? Oh, yes, yes. Very nice. Now, let's go.'

Jess and Leanne exchanged rolling eyes which told it all. Jess decided if her father ever said she just looked *nice* on her wedding day she would throttle him.

Thinking of her own future wedding day thoroughly distracted Jess as they made their way from the house over to the rose garden, making her only dimly aware of her surrounds. She'd done her best to put a halt to her escalating feelings for Ben during the hours she'd spent with him earlier on, focusing on the physical and not the emotional. But her heart had been as impossible to control as her body. It had soared every time she'd touched him. But it had been performing oral sex on him which had been the killer. She had loved the way he'd lost control under her mouth and hands. He hadn't wanted to, she was sure. But he'd seemed as powerless to stop himself as she'd been. Not that that meant anything. She wasn't that naïve.

They'd used the only remaining condom in no time, with a still turned-on Jess eventually offering to go and get the condom she kept in her bag which was in the other bedroom. Ben had followed her there, pulling her down onto the rug by the bed where he'd taken her on all fours, squeezing her nipples as she came. It was the first time in her life that she'd had sex that way and she'd loved it, giving rise to the hope that she wasn't falling in love, just suffering from an intense case of lust.

Ben had been wrong about their not actually sleeping. When he'd carried her back to bed after that rather rough mating on the floor, she'd passed out, not waking till Ben had started shaking her shoulder.

'Oh, Lord!' she'd exclaimed, sitting bolt upright and pushing her tangled hair out of her eyes. 'What time is it?' Ben was dressed, she'd immediately noted. Not in what he would be wearing at the wedding. Just jeans and a top.

'Shortly before two-thirty. Andy will be here any moment. You said you had to do your hair.'

Jess had grimaced. 'I'll have to shampoo it again. It's a mess.'

Just then there'd been a knock on the front door, Andy calling out as he'd opened it and walked into the hallway. Panicked, Jess had grabbed a sheet to cover herself, Ben unable to get to the open doorway in time before Andy had been standing in it.

'Oh, sorry,' Andy had said hurriedly on seeing an obviously naked Jess in the bed. 'I'll…er…wait for you outside, Ben.'

'No sweat.' He'd turned to throw Jess an apologetic glance. 'Sorry about that, my darling. See you at the wedding.'

Jess recalled that her heart had turned over at his calling her his darling. It turned over again when she caught sight of him standing with Andy at the end of the strip of red carpet which had been rolled out between the rows of decorated seats. No doubt the groom and the other groomsman looked almost as good as Ben in their black dinner suits. But Jess didn't see anyone or anything else but him, smiling at her. Talk about tunnel vision!

Some taped wedding music started up and she floated down the makeshift aisle, unaware of the admiring whispers from the guests, aware of nothing but Ben's eyes upon her.

Bloody hell, Ben thought as Jess walked slowly towards them. *She is just so damned desirable!*

'You are one lucky guy, mate,' Andy murmured out of the side of his mouth. 'That is one hot babe.'

'You ought to talk,' Ben managed to whisper back when the bride finally came into view. But he hardly noticed Catherine or heard the ceremony. He just went through the motions, producing the rings on cue, thankful that it was a relatively short service. He could not wait to be alone with Jess again.

His first opportunity to speak to her was at the signing of the register which they did to one side after Catherine and Andy had been declared man and wife.

'You look very pretty in pink,' he whispered as he passed her the pen. 'But I prefer you in nothing.'

He noticed her hand trembling as she signed her name. It excited him, the way he could turn her on like that. She wasn't like other girls he'd slept with. She seemed less experienced and more capable of being surprised. That, in itself, was very arousing. The temptation to push her sexual boundaries was acute, especially since she was obviously a highly sexed girl. She'd loved going down on him. He'd loved it too. It worried Ben, though, the tendency he had to lose control with her on occasion.

Next time, he would not let that happen. Ben had a penchant for erotic fun and games, first sparked when he'd had an affair with an older woman during his university days. She'd been a mature student who liked being dominated in bed, teaching Ben all there was to know about such role playing. Ben had enjoyed playing lord and master to the hilt. He still did. Ben already had an idea in mind for tonight, an idea which he hoped Jess would go along with. He felt pretty sure that she would.

Damn, but it was going to an excruciatingly long evening!

Jess could not believe how long the evening proved to be. The photos had been tedious, as had the serving and eating of the three-course meal. It wasn't till coffee and cheeses were served that Ben finally stood up to make the best man speech.

He didn't look at all nervous. Which irritated her. Perhaps because it underlined how confident a person he was. Which was perverse. Hadn't she told him she liked confident men?

She actually didn't mind *liking* Ben. She would never have had sex with him if she hadn't liked him. She just didn't want to fall in love with him.

'Ladies and gentlemen,' Ben began. 'Firstly, let me thank you all for coming here today to celebrate Andy's marriage to Catherine who, might I say, is the most beautiful bride I have ever seen.'

Not just confident, Jess thought ruefully, but a silver-tongued charmer.

'For those who don't know me personally, you might be wondering what a chap with an American accent is doing as Andy's best man. Trust me when I say I might sound like a Yank, but if you scratch the surface you will find an Aussie through and through.'

Cheering from the guests.

'Andy and I go way back. He was my best friend all through boarding school and then through law school. He was always there for me. Always. And I love him. Sorry, Andy, I know you don't like mushy. Now, I know it is traditional to embarrass the groom by telling stories of things he got up to in his pre-wed life, but I have struggled to think of anything which Andy ever did which was stupid or reckless. Of course, I have been living in the US of A for the past ten years, so perhaps a few potential slip-ups have eluded me. I did hear a rumour that when he was in France he burnt the candle at both ends, so to speak.'

Laughter from the guests.

Ben smiled. 'But I do not believe a word of it. From what I saw last night at Andy's stag party, his candle is still in full working order.'

More laughter from the guests. And a horrified glance from the bride.

'Just kidding, Catherine. Andy's was the best behaved stag party I have ever attended. On a serious note, folks, believe me when I say that Andy is the most sensible, smartest man I have ever known. It's testimony to his brain power that he has chosen such a lovely girl as Catherine as his life partner. They are a well-matched couple who love each other dearly. Such love is a precious gift, one which should be treasured. And protected. And toasted. So, will you please all be upstanding and charge your glasses...'

Everyone obeyed, especially Jess, who had been moved by the last part of Ben's speech. Love was indeed precious, especially true love. Colin hadn't truly loved her. As for Ben... No point in going there!

'To Andy and Catherine,' Ben said loudly as he held up his own glass.

All the guests repeated his words as they clinked glasses and drank.

Jess did likewise, then sat back down, feeling suddenly drained. More speeches followed and, finally, Andy stood up to speak. He did not have Ben's gift of the gab, or the same smooth delivery, but what he said was sweet and touching. It actually brought tears to Jess's eyes, which she had to blink back swiftly when he proposed a toast to the bridesmaids, explaining how Jess had had to step in at the last moment and how grateful they were to her.

Jess sat there, her right hand fingering the lovely silver and diamond pendant Andy had given the bridesmaids earlier. Catherine had received a magnificent pair of diamond-drop earrings. When Jess had insisted to Catherine that they give her pendant to Krissie afterwards, Catherine had said no, she and Andy would buy Krissie something special for the baby when it came.

They really were a very nice couple. And, yes, very much in love. Jess couldn't help envying them their happiness. She was no longer pleased that Ben planned to stay in Australia a little longer. She knew the score. He wanted hot sex with her after which he would wing his way back to New York and forget she ever existed. And by then, she could very well be left behind with a broken heart.

Common sense demanded she have no more to do with Ben after this weekend was over. But common sense was no match for the sexual heat which had been charging through her veins ever since they'd signed the marriage certificate together. A few hot words whispered in her ear and she had almost combusted on the spot. Her still-erect nipples burned as they pressed against the satin lining of her dress, her belly tight with sexual tension. She couldn't wait for this reception to be over so she could be with Ben again. She could not wait!

But she *had* to wait, she accepted wretchedly. Dear God, but she was in over her head here with this man.

At last they moved along to the cake-cutting part. Soon would come the bridal waltz, after which the serious partying would begin. Though tempted, Jess decided not to drink too much, so there wouldn't be a problem with driving back to the cottage as soon as they could leave.

Which wouldn't be any time soon, Jess realised with some dismay. No way could the best man leave till the bride and groom had gone—only a couple of hours to go, but it seemed like an eternity.

'Care for a dance, ma'am?' asked a voice with a thick, southern accent.

Jess's head jerked around to find Ben standing behind her chair with a goofy smile on his face.

'They say a fella's best chance to get lucky at a wedding is with one of the bridesmaids,' he added, acting like some redneck out of the hills.

Jess had to smile. *He* obviously hadn't been sitting there, all churned up. This was all just fun and games to him!

'Well, I sure wouldn't want to disappoint a fella as handsome as you,' she returned saucily. There was no point in being a wet blanket. Though dancing with him was going to be sheer torture.

'Aw, shucks, ma'am,' Ben returned, twisting his hands

together in fake embarrassment. 'You shouldn't say things like that to a shy boy from Alabama.'

Jess laughed as she stood up. 'Now you sound like a character from one of those Doris Day, Rock Hudson movies.'

'Yeah, I know,' he said, dropping the fake southern accent as he steered her onto the dance floor. 'Those old movies have a way of drawing you in. I gather you like them too,' he added, and pulled her into his arms.

Jess melted into him and closed her eyes, savouring the feel of his body against hers whilst trying to contain her ever-increasing excitement.

'Mum does,' she said. 'I sometimes watch one with her. She likes happy endings.'

'And you? What kind of movies do you like?'

Oh, Lord, now he wanted to chat! She tried not to sigh. 'I guess something which is both entertainment and escape. I don't go to the movies to watch things that are too real. I can't stand stories about drug dealers or war or people who are mean and cruel.'

'You like reading?'

'I'm not as avid a reader as Mum. I spend a lot of my spare time sewing. But I do like a good thriller.'

'Romances?'

'One or two. I did read a certain erotic romance which swept the world by storm.'

'And did it give you a few delicious ideas?' he murmured against her ear.

She shivered as his lips made contact, his tongue tip dipping inside. But only for a split second.

She groaned softly when his head lifted, suppressing another groan when the other groomsman, Jay, tapped Ben on the shoulder and suggested they change partners.

Ben no more wanted to dance with Leanne than fly a

kite, but what could he do? He'd been brought up to be polite, to have proper manners. So he smiled and handed Jess over to Jay whilst he did his duty and danced with the very silly Leanne.

'So, how long have you known Jess?' was the first thing Leanne said, her voice as curious as her eyes.

'Not that long,' he replied, his own eyes drifting over to where Jay was holding Jess too darned close, in his opinion.

'She's very attractive, isn't she?' Leanne went on.

Ben agreed.

'Girls like that can get any man they want,' she said with an envious sounding sigh.

Ben thought of Colin doing a flit but didn't mention him.

Leanne fluttered her eyes up at him. 'It must be difficult for a really rich man like you to know if a girl likes him for himself or his money.'

Ben was astonished at the sly bitchiness behind Leanne's remark. 'I'm not that rich, Leanne.'

Leanne smiled a knowing smile. 'Maybe not now but you will be one day. I mean, your daddy's a billionaire, according to Catherine. Not that I think Jess is a gold-digger. She's a very sweet girl.'

'You're certainly right there,' Ben stated, thinking to himself that Leanne was a nasty piece of work. Of all the girls he'd ever been with, Jess was the *least* likely to be with him for his money. If anything, his wealth was a mark against him. Hadn't she said she would never marry a man as rich as he was?

It was a relief when Andy tapped him on the shoulder and handed him over to Catherine. Let *him* put up with Leanne's malicious prattle. He'd had enough of her for one night. Ben had to smile, however, when within less than a minute Andy whirled Leanne over to Jay and gave her back to him, happily dancing with Jess instead.

Which made Ben happy as well. He didn't mind Jess dancing with Andy. He certainly hadn't liked her dancing with Jay. Hadn't liked another man holding her that close and possibly trying to crack onto her.

Ben frowned as he realised just how possessive he was beginning to feel about Jess. It wasn't like him to be jealous. He'd always despised that kind of self-destructive emotion. But with Jess he just didn't have the control over his emotions that he usually had. He didn't have as much control over his body either.

It had been a battle to stop himself from having an erection all evening, finally losing the war when he'd taken her in his arms just now. Not that anything showed. His dinner jacket covered the evidence of his almost obsessive desire. But he could *feel* it, damn it. Not just in his flesh, but in his mind. Never had he wanted a woman as much as he wanted Jess. He could not wait to strip that infernal dress off her and do all the things he wanted to do to her.

CHAPTER FIFTEEN

'THANK GOD THEY'RE GONE,' Ben muttered under his breath as Andy and Catherine drove off in their much-decorated car. The happy couple were spending their wedding night in a nearby, very swanky guest house, which was fortunate, given Andy had imbibed quite a lot of champagne. Ben hadn't touched a drop; he needed a clear head and an un-intoxicated body for the games he had in mind for Jess tonight. It possibly would be the last opportunity to indulge himself with her in such a fashion. He did have full access to his mother's apartment at Blue Bay tomorrow night—she didn't get back till Monday—but Jess might not be willing to stay the night with him there. It was obvious that she still lived at home and still had to answer to her parents. Her mother, anyway.

Meanwhile…

Jess spotted Ben standing at the edge of the throng of guests who'd gone outside to watch the bride and groom depart. He'd been in a distracted mood the last hour or so. Not talking much. Not drinking either. She'd kept her consumption to a minimum, but then she had to drive. He didn't.

When she came up to him, he was frowning.

'Why are you frowning like that?' she asked him. 'Is your shoulder aching?' She wouldn't put it past him to have lied to her about his arm. Men hated to admit to any weakness, especially physical ones.

'No,' he said, giving her an odd look. 'It's fine. And more than capable of giving you a good spanking when the time comes.'

Jess sucked in sharply. 'Spanking?' she repeated in shocked tones even as the picture of her being bent naked over his thighs zoomed into her mind.

She stared up at him, her whole head whirling as she tried to work out if the idea excited or repulsed her.

'I think you might enjoy the experience. But only if you want me to, Jess,' he continued in that soft, seductive voice he often adopted. 'I would never force you to do anything you didn't want to do.'

But that was the problem, wasn't it? Once he started on her, she wanted to do whatever he wanted to. Already she was wondering what it would feel like to be spanked.

Jess struggled to act cool when she was anything but. 'I…I'll think about it,' she said. And of course that was another problem. Thinking about doing sexual things with him invariably turned her on. She was already turned on. Had been all evening. Now, her body temperature and her desire metre were zooming off the charts.

'Come on,' he said brusquely. 'Let's get out of here.'

Jess hesitated. 'But shouldn't we say goodbye to people first?'

'Who do you have in mind? We'll see Glen and Heather in the morning before we leave. We can say goodbye to them then.'

'But we won't see the bride's parents in the morning. We should say goodbye to them. It's only polite.'

Ben grimaced. 'You can, if you like. I can't stand either of them. I'll wait here for you. Don't be long.'

She whirled away from him and raced back into the

marquee, taking less than five minutes to say the appropriate goodbyes and collect her bouquet. He was still looking impatient when she returned to his side.

'What took you so long?' he growled as he steered her in the direction of the main house and her parked SUV.

She could not contain a surge of exasperation, shrugging off his bruising hold and grinding to a halt. 'For pity's sake, Ben, what's got into you all of a sudden? You're acting like a jerk.'

He sighed. 'Sorry. Just impatient to be alone with you, that's all.'

'Oh.' Trust him to say the one thing guaranteed to defuse her anger.

'Do you have your keys with you?' he asked when they approached her vehicle.

'Yes, of course.'

'Good. Now, get in and drive.'

She got in, tossed her bouquet in the back, then drove, all conversation between them ceasing during the five minutes it took to negotiate the short trip back to the cottage. By the time she pulled up in front of the small porch, her stomach was churning and her heart was pounding behind her ribs.

Was she really going to let him spank her?

Oh, Lord, she thought, and let out a panicky rush of air.

Ben heard her ragged sigh and recognised the reason behind it.

'Don't be nervous,' he said gently.

'I am a bit. I've never been spanked before.'

'I gathered that. Have you ever been tied up before?'

Her eyes went like saucers. 'No. I…I thought they only did things like that in books and in brothels.'

'Lots of real people like to play erotic games. Which is all I'm suggesting. Nothing serious. I'm not into humiliation or pain. I just want to give you pleasure, Jess. You can say no at any stage to anything you don't like.'

'But…but I might not know that I don't like it till you've done it.'

'I see.' God, but she was delightful. And delicious. And he wanted her like crazy. 'I promise to take things slowly, then. Give you time to say no before things go too far.'

'Oh. All right.'

'Let's go.'

He took her into the bathroom first where he undressed her—slowly, as he'd promised. The sight of her fiercely erect nipples revealed that she was genuinely enjoying herself. So far. She gasped when he tweaked one of the pink peaks, then groaned when he did the same to the other one.

'Still a little tender?' he enquired as he quickly disposed of his own clothes.

'A little,' she confessed shakily.

'But not too tender,' he said, and she shook her head.

'Good. Here, I think I should take off that diamond pendant as well. We wouldn't want it to get broken, would we?'

Her head whirled whilst he undid the clasp, then placed the pendant on the vanity along with his expensive looking wrist-watch. He hadn't taken his watch off last night, she recalled. But then he hadn't spanked her last night.

Oh, God.

Her heartbeat went up another notch.

'We'll have a shower together first,' he said. 'But no touching from you, beautiful. You are *way* too good with your hands.'

Ben turned her back to him whilst he washed her, making her moan when he rubbed the soapy sponge back and forth between her legs, her peach-like buttocks clenching tightly together when he moved his attention to them. By the time he switched off the water and turned her to face him, he knew she was ready for him to do whatever he wanted. Her eyes were glazed over and her lips had fallen apart as she panted for breath.

Ben thought she had never looked more beautiful or more desirable. He almost decided to bypass the foreplay in favour of straightforward sex but he suspected Jess was by now looking forward to the experience. Ben could only hope that he would be able to control himself during what was usually a lengthy game.

He stepped out of the cubicle and reached for the two white towelling robes which were hanging on the back of the door. After putting one on, he handed the other robe to Jess.

'Put that on,' he ordered.

When she did so without question, he wanted her all the more.

'No, don't do it up,' he said, and reached for the sash, sliding it through the side loops before wrapping it around his left wrist.

He had to take her hand and lead her back to the bedroom. By the time they got to the side of the bed, she was trembling. But he felt certain it was no longer from nerves.

'You should be dry by now. So you won't be needing that robe.'

'But you've still got yours on,' she protested.

'That's the idea.'

When she hesitated, he bent and whispered in her ear. 'Yours is not to reason why, Jess. Yours is just to lie back on that bed and let me give you pleasure.'

His breathing quickened as she obediently took off the robe and lay down on the bed, her head on the pillows.

'No, not that way,' he said and she just stared at him, sucking in sharply when he turned her over onto her stomach.

'Just say no if you want me to stop,' he said.

She didn't say no, but she did bury her face in the pillow.

Gently, he took both her hands and placed them in the small of her back, then looped her wrists together with the sash from the robe. Not tightly, but enough so that she would feel bound and helpless. Which was the point, of course. That was what would excite her to fever pitch. Finally, he removed the pillow from under her face and slid it under her hips, raising her buttocks in the most erotic and inviting fashion.

When Ben stepped back to examine his handiwork, the sight of her like that took his breath away. Dear God, she was just so sexy looking. And totally at his mercy! It was a heady combination. And, whilst he was fiercely erect, all of a sudden Ben wasn't so concerned about his own satisfaction but how Jess was feeling. He hated to think she might be afraid to say no at this stage.

'Are you all right, Jess?' he asked softly. 'Do you want me to continue?'

CHAPTER SIXTEEN

Was he insane? She would die if he didn't continue. She'd never been so excited in her whole life!

'I'm fine,' she said, her voice high-pitched and raspy. 'Please don't stop.'

He laughed a short, sexy laugh. 'Your wish is my command.'

Now *that* was a laugh, Jess thought. *He* was the one doing the commanding. But didn't she just love it!

No touching from you, beautiful... Put that on... You won't be needing that robe.... Just lie back on that bed and let me give you pleasure...

'It's just a game, Jess,' he said. 'You can stop me at any time. Okay?'

'Okay,' she mumbled.

The first crack of his hand on her right buttock brought a gasp of shock, rather than pain. Though it did sting. Jess buried her face into the quilt, determined not to cry out again. Another slap followed. Then another, his hand moving from left to right in a slow, relentless rhythm till both her buttocks were burning. And red, no doubt. Yet despite her discomfort—oh, yes, her whole bottom was stinging like mad—she didn't want to tell him to stop. There was something exquisitely pleasurable in the whole experience. She held her breath between slaps in anticipation of his large palm making contact with her soft skin, biting her bottom lip each time it happened. The slaps began coming at a slower interval now, her time of waiting extended till she almost pleaded for more. When he finally stopped altogether, she groaned in frustration.

'That's enough,' she heard him say.

But he didn't untie her. Instead, the bed dipped as he lay down beside her. She saw he was naked now when she twisted her head to look at him.

'So what did you think?' he asked her.

'I think,' she choked out, 'that if you don't have sex with me in the next ten seconds, then you're a dead man.'

He smiled. 'You're not really in a position to give orders right now, are you, darling Jess?'

'Ben,' she said pleadingly. 'Please.'

'If you insist.'

She couldn't believe it when he didn't untie her first, just spread her legs wide and moved around between them. She moaned when he rubbed his tip against her, her teeth digging into her lower lip to stop herself from screaming.

'So wet,' he muttered.

Ben was close to losing it. Time to get a condom on, he realised, before things got out of hand.

Thank God Andy had given him a good supply so he had one at the ready.

She cried out when he entered her, her bottom moving frantically against him with an urgency which betrayed a cruel level of frustration. He wasn't much better, grabbing her hips with bruising fingers and setting up a savage rhythm, forgetting everything but what his flesh was feeling at that moment. The heat. The urgent need. The madness of it all. Her stunningly violent climax only preceeded his by a second or two, Ben thrilling to the way she cried out as she came.

Jess lay there afterwards, stunned yet totally sated. A draining languor started seeping into her limbs, her eyelids growing heavier and heavier. Ben was lying across her back, his own breathing now slow and heavy. She desperately wanted to stay awake. But sleep would not be denied. It came quickly, with Jess's wrists still bound.

Ben fell asleep too, still slumped across her back.

He woke first, momentarily confused by where he was. And then he remembered. Everything.

He groaned as guilt consumed him. How could he possibly have left her that way? She didn't wake as he carefully withdrew, then even more carefully untied her. She stirred slightly when he slid the pillow out from under her hips, but she didn't wake, thank God, though she did curl herself up into a semi-foetal position. After throwing a sheet over her far too delicious derrière, he headed for the bathroom.

A quick shower later and he was back in the bedroom, standing at the side of the bed and staring down at her still body. Ben supposed he really had nothing to be guilty about; Jess had obviously enjoyed herself. Ben was never absolutely sure if his girlfriends went along with his demands because they were genuinely on the same sexual wavelength or because he was Morgan De Silva's son and heir. He definitely had no such doubts with Jess. Damn it, but he wished she lived in America.

Maybe he would ask her to go back with him. He could get her a job and lease her a nice little apartment. Or she could even move in with him.

Ben frowned at this last thought. His father had warned him never to do that: have a woman move in with him. Not unless they were married. As much as Jess claimed she would never marry a rich man, she hadn't seen his New York lifestyle. His thirty-square apartment overlooking Central Park had a lap pool on the roof plus a fully equipped gym and spa room. He had a wardrobe full of designer suits and hand-made shoes, a Ferrari in the underground car park and an expense account which allowed him to dine at all of New York's finest restaurants. He also had access to the company's private jet which flew him to Acapulco for weekends in the summer and Aspen in the winter.

That kind of lifestyle could corrupt even the nicest girl, especially if she'd never experienced such luxury. Which Jess obviously hadn't.

No, best not ask her to go back to America with him. Best he do what he'd originally intended: have a holiday fling with Jess, then leave it at that. It wasn't as though he was in love with her. He just liked and admired her a lot. And wanted her like mad. Already he had another erection, tempting him to climb back into bed and wake her. He didn't think she'd mind.

Ben sensibly armed himself with protection first, then climbed in under the sheet and curved his body around hers, spoon fashion. She stirred immediately, stiffening against him when he began to caress her breasts. Obviously they were still sensitive from all the attention he'd been giving them, so he moved lower, stroking her stomach, then her thighs.

'Yes please,' she choked out when he pressed himself against her still-wet sex.

A wave of tenderness engulfed Ben as he slid into her. God, but he'd never felt anything like this for a girl before. She was just so sweet, yet so sexy at the same time. A girl in a million.

He took his time, setting up a gentle rhythm, loving the sounds she made, loving the way she wriggled against him as her excitement grew. And, when he knew he was close to coming himself, he touched her in a way that would guarantee her release as well.

They came together, Ben startled as another wave of emotion hit him. Not just tenderness this time, but something deeper. Much deeper. He held her tightly in his arms afterwards and wondered if he was finally on the verge of falling in love.

CHAPTER SEVENTEEN

JESS WAS WOKEN by Ben shaking her shoulder again, plus the sound of her phone ringing.

'I was in the kitchen making coffee when it rang,' he explained as he handed it to her.

Jess tried to take the phone, sit up and cover her bare breasts at the same time, but failed.

What the heck? she thought despairingly. It wasn't anything he hadn't seen before. Yet, strangely, she felt shy in front of Ben all of a sudden. Jess supposed it wasn't every day that one woke to such memories. In a way, it didn't seem real. Had she really let him tie her up and spank her? Obviously she had, if her still-tender bottom was anything to go by.

'It's my mother,' she said, trying to look and sound cool. 'Would you mind?' She waved him away.

He smiled, turned and left the room. Thank God. The infernal man was stark naked. Obviously, he never suffered from shyness.

'Hello, Mum,' she said into the phone. 'It's a little early, isn't it? I've only just woken up. Can I tell you all about the wedding when I get home?'

'I guess so. But, before you go, I was also ringing to remind you that today is family barbecue day. I thought you might have forgotten.'

She had, actually. It was a once a month tradition where the family got together at her parents' place.

'I was thinking that you could ask Ben to come along. Your father and I would love to meet him.'

Meaning *she'd* like to see what he looked like. Her mother was a very intuitive woman and had probably picked up something from Jess's voice.

'I'll ask him, Mum,' she said. 'But I won't guarantee that he'll say yes. He might just want to get home after such a long drive.'

'I see. Well, how about you call me when you stop and tell me if Ben's coming or not?'

'Will do. Now, I must go, Mum.'

'Before you go, did the wedding go off all right yester-day? No other Murphy's Law disasters?'

'Everything was perfect, Mum,' she said. 'I'll ring you later. Bye.'

Rising, Jess dashed for the bathroom, where the sight of her pink bridesmaid dress draped over the bath reminded her of the submissive scenario Ben had insisted upon in there. That was where her loss of will-power had all started, of course. In that shower. By the time he'd turned off the water, she'd been so excited that he could have done anything to her and she would not have objected.

The speed with which he'd turned her into a submis-sive sex slave was quite shocking. So why wasn't she more shocked this morning? Maybe it was because underneath all that S&M role-playing Ben was a nice man. A decent man. She felt confident that he would never hurt her for real. Look at the way he'd made love to her later in the night, so gently and rather sweetly. She'd enjoyed that time even more than all the other times so far. And there'd been quite a few already, Jess thought ruefully. Ben couldn't seem to keep his hands off her. In more ways than one!

After a rather quick shower, Jess rubbed some of the body lotion she found in the vanity into her buttocks. They were still a little on the tender side, but nothing major. Once her teeth were cleaned and her hair up in a pony-tail, she hurried into the other bedroom where she took out some fresh clothes: a pair of three-quarter length white trousers and a navy-and-white striped top. Slipping white sandals onto her feet, she headed for the kitchen where Ben was thankfully now wearing the white bathrobe which had been on the bedroom floor earlier. He was sitting at the kitchen table with some toast and coffee in front of him.

'I think your mother's checking up on you,' he said.

'Possibly. It's hard to put anything past my mum.'

'Not for the want of your trying, though,' he said, smil-ing at her.

Lord, but he was devilishly attractive when he smiled like that, even with slightly bleary eyes and a stubbly chin.

'She wanted to know how the wedding went. And to invite you to our family barbecue tonight.'

His eyebrows lifted, then fell. 'Do *you* want me to go, Jess?'

She shrugged. 'I doubt you'll enjoy it much. Mum will give you the once-over, then Dad'll probably give you the third degree, if he thinks you're interested in me.'

'Which I am.'

It annoyed Jess, his saying that. Because he wasn't re-ally interested in her in that way. He just wanted to have more sex with her whilst he was here in Australia. Okay, so Ben was basically a good man, but he was also spoiled and selfish. It wasn't all his fault, of course. He'd been born beautiful and into great wealth: both very corrupting fac-tors. He'd probably developed his liking for kinky sex be-cause he'd had so much sex in his life he'd got bored with straightforward love-making. Which was a pity. Because he did straightforward love-making very well indeed.

Jess sighed. 'I honestly don't think you should go.'

'Why not?'

'For the reasons I just told you.'

'But I want to meet your parents.'

Jess rolled her eyes. 'For pity's sake, *why*?'

'Because I want to ask them to give you this week off so we can go to Sydney and work together on Fab Fashions. I thought we might stay down there instead of driving up and down the motorway every day. Mum has a flat in Bondi we could use.'

Jess didn't know what to say. She wanted to go, of course. Wanted the opportunity to do something about Fab Fashions. And, yes, she wanted to spend more time alone with Ben, especially some more of his very exciting brand of sex. She'd be lying if she didn't admit that, especially to herself. But at the back of her mind, in that place reserved for difficult decisions, she knew if she did this, then she was sure to become even more emotionally involved with him.

'I...I don't know, Ben,' she said hesitantly, turning away to make herself some coffee. 'Like you said, there's probably no fixing Fab Fashions. We'd just be wasting our time.'

'I don't agree. We'll have that chat on the drive home and come up with a new name, one which will lend itself to a successful marketing strategy. Because you're right, Jess. Companies like ours shouldn't just bail out when things get tough. We can afford to ride some losses for a while, especially when the alternative means that people will lose their jobs.'

Jess wanted to believe he meant it. But she didn't. Companies like De Silva & Associates were all about making profits. They didn't give a damn about the little people. Which was what she was. One of the little people.

Jess finished making her coffee, then carried it over to the table. 'I'm sorry, Ben,' she said, pulling out a chair and sitting down, 'but I'd rather not. I'm a mechanic, not some marketing expert.'

'So you're giving up on Fab Fashions?'

'I've told you what's wrong with the business. You're an intelligent man. I'll put my thinking cap on during the drive back and come up with a name which might suit. Then it's up to you to do something with it.'

He looked at her long and hard, then shrugged. 'Okay. If that's the way you want it.'

What she wanted at that moment was never to have met Ben De Silva.

'I still wouldn't mind coming to that barbecue, Jess.'

'No, Ben. I'd rather you didn't.'

He frowned at her. 'Why is that?'

'I don't want my parents knowing what we've been up to this weekend. And they will. Mum will take one look at us together and she'll know.'

'We're consenting adults, Jess. Our having sex isn't a crime.'

'No, but it's very unlike me, Ben, to hop into bed so quickly. Mum's sure to jump to the wrong conclusion.'

'Which is?

'That I've fallen madly in love.'

Again, she was on the end of another long, thoughtful look.

'I take it that hasn't happened?'

'You know it hasn't. We've been having a dirty weekend, Ben. That's all.' It went against her grain to describe their weekend in such a crude fashion, but it was the truth after all.

'I don't see it that way, Jess. I like you. A lot. And I want to see more of you.'

'You mean you want to have more kinky sex with me whilst you're in Australia.'

He pursed his lips in obvious annoyance. 'You make it all sound so tacky. Yes, of course I want to have more sex with you, but not just kinky sex. I enjoy making love to you in more traditional ways as well. I also want to spend time with you out of bed.'

Jess's laugh was a little bitter. 'Yes, I noticed you like having sex out of bed too.'

His blue eyes flashed with frustration. 'Very funny. Just remember, you're the one who knocked back my offer of our working together on Fab Fashions.'

'I can live with that. I can't live with you taking me for a fool.'

He sat bolt upright in his chair, his face furious. 'I would never do that. I think you're one of the smartest girls I've ever met. And the most stubborn. I suppose if I asked you to go back to New York with me, you'd say no to that as well!'

Jess could not have been more taken aback. Or more speechless.

'Well?' he snapped when she said nothing. 'What *would* you say to such an offer?'

Jess gathered in a deep breath, then let it out slowly. 'I would say thank you very much, Ben, but no thank you. My life is here, in Australia. I wouldn't be happy in New York.'

'How do you know?'

'I just know.'

His eyes carried exasperation. 'Most girls would jump at the chance. For Pete's sake, Jess, you wouldn't have to pay for a thing. You could stay in my apartment and have the holiday of a lifetime.'

The word 'holiday' reaffirmed what Jess already knew. He wasn't seriously interested in her. Not the way she would have liked. But then, that was never going to happen. He'd already said he didn't want to get married. She was just a passing amusement, one which he hadn't grown bored with yet.

'Couldn't we just leave things the way they are, Ben? I'm happy to go out with you whilst you're staying up on the coast. I like you a lot, but I don't want to go to America with you.'

Ben should have been relieved, he supposed, that she hadn't jumped at his somewhat impulsive offer. But he wasn't. He was bitterly disappointed. He'd wanted to show her New York, wanted to give her the time of her life.

'Fine,' he bit out.

'Please don't think me ungrateful, Ben,' she went on, her eyes softening on him. 'It was a very generous offer. But it's best I stay here in Australia.'

He sighed, then smiled at her. 'So we're still on for dinner tomorrow night?'

Jess smiled back at him. 'Of course. Where are you going to take me?'

'I have no idea. I'll ask Mum when she gets back tomorrow. She knows all the best local restaurants. But you'll have to pick me up. I'm not allowed to drive till I get that stupid medical clearance. Hopefully by Tuesday that'll be done and I can drive Mum's car.'

'So your mother will be there when I pick you up?' she said, sounding a bit panicky.

'Yes, but you don't have to worry. Mum's really quite nice, despite everything.'

'What do you mean by that?'

'I'll explain on the drive back,' he said, thinking he shouldn't have made such a leading comment. But it was too late now. Besides, it would give them something to talk about. Telling Jess all about his mother's exploits over the years would take some time. 'I'll go shower and shave whilst you have breakfast. Then we should get going.'

CHAPTER EIGHTEEN

BY THE TIME they stopped at Sandy Hollow for lunch, Jess had a much better understanding of why Ben wasn't interested in marriage. To find out that your mother had married your father for his money must have come as a bitter blow. Still, it had been good of his father not to say anything till Ben had turned twenty-one. That way, Ben had been able to grow up loving his mother who, though materialistic, had obviously been a good mother to him.

Despite that, Jess could just imagine how Ben had felt when his mother had admitted she'd trapped his father into marriage with a pregnancy and had never loved him. His money was what she'd loved. Yes, there were reasons for her materialism, but the bottom line was still not very nice. Her actions certainly wouldn't have engendered faith in her son's own relationships with the opposite sex. Given he would one day be as rich as his father, Ben would always be on the lookout for signs that his girlfriends were gold-diggers. Which was an awful way to have to live.

But it did also explain why Ben concentrated on sex when he was with a girl he liked. Sex was safe, especially the kind of sex he indulged in. Such goings-on kept his girlfriends at a distance, both physically and emotionally. Jess realised that the only time he'd had sex face to face with her had been when she'd been on top. But even then he'd adopted the role of voyeur rather than that of a loving partner.

'Neither of your parents have married again,' she remarked once they sat down to another pub lunch. Different pub but similar food. A steak sandwich and salad. 'Why is that, do you think?'

Ben shrugged. 'Mum always said she would marry again if she ever fell in love. But that's unlikely to happen, given the type of man she usually dates—all young, handsome studs without much between their ears. Mum does like intelligence when she's out of bed.'

Jess tried not to look shocked at his talking about his mother's sex life in that fashion.

'But who knows? This fellow she's gone on the cruise with seems a different kettle of fish. Not so young and he actually works. I'll find out more when she gets home tomorrow. As far as Dad is concerned... This might sound silly but I think Mum was the only woman Dad ever truly loved. Though don't get me wrong. He was unfaithful to her during their marriage. Had several mistresses going at once, apparently. He still has women running after him, despite being sixty-five and not the best-looking man in the world. Money is a powerful aphrodisiac,' he added drily.

Jess sighed. 'I can understand now why you don't want to get married.'

'What?' Ben said, almost knocking his drink over. 'I never said I didn't want to get married.'

Jess frowned. 'But you did. When I asked you why you broke up with Amber you said she wanted marriage and you didn't.'

'Not with *her* I don't. I don't love her. That doesn't mean I wouldn't consider it with anyone else at some stage.'

'Oh,' Jess said, startled by this turn of events. Not that

it changed anything. Ben might want marriage at some stage, but it wouldn't be to an ordinary girl like her.

Ben stared across the table at Jess and wondered if that was why she'd refused to come to New York with him. Because she wanted marriage and she thought he didn't. Not that he was about to propose. He did, however, feel more strongly about Jess than any girl he'd ever met.

He decided then and there that he would ask her to come to New York with him again later in the week. Meanwhile, he'd show her the time of her life every night. And, yes, behind the scenes he'd even do something about that damned Fab Fashions.

'Are you absolutely sure you don't want me to come to your family barbecue?' he asked coolly before picking up his steak sandwich and taking a big bite.

She was tempted. He could see she was tempted.

'I promise to be on my best behaviour,' he added once his mouth was temporarily empty.

She laughed. 'It's not you I'm worried about. It's my mother.'

Ben didn't give a damn if her mother realised they were sleeping together. Mothers had never been a problem to him. They usually liked him a lot. 'I can handle your mother,' he said.

Lord, but he was an arrogant devil. But she did so like him. And she wanted him like mad. Already she was regretting not going to New York with him, even if it *was* only for a holiday. Still, she suspected Ben hadn't totally given up on that idea. Jess wondered what she would say if he asked her again.

Hopefully, she would have the courage—and the common sense—still to say no. But, dear Lord, she did have a lot of trouble saying no to him.

'I'm coming to that barbecue,' he announced firmly,

'And that's final. Now, about that new name for Fab Fashions; I've given it some thought. What do you think of Real Women? It would lend itself to a good advertising campaign. Clothes for real women, et cetera, et cetera.'

The take-over man in action again, Jess thought. Telling her he was coming, then changing the subject.

She had to smile. He was clever all right.

'I think it's a great name,' she said. 'I love it.'

He beamed across the table at her. '*Finally* she agrees with something I've suggested!'

'I can be agreeable,' she said. 'When it's a sensible suggestion.'

'Coming to New York with me is just as sensible.'

'Ben,' she said with a warning look. 'Just leave it, will you?'

'Okay. I will. For now. But I make no promise to do so indefinitely.'

They both fell to eating their meals, Jess doing her best to stop thinking about her potentially dangerous feelings for Ben. Once again she wished she could be like other girls. Most would jump at the chance of going to New York with him, even if it didn't lead to anything permanent.

But maybe it would; she started hoping as she ate. How would she know unless she agreed? She'd gone to bed with Ben initially because she knew she'd regret it if she didn't. Maybe she'd regret not going to New York with him and not giving their relationship a chance.

But it *wasn't* a relationship, her more pragmatic side argued. It was just a fling, or an affair, for want of a better word. Ben had never said he loved her. Not that he would. It was way too early for a man of his natural wariness to make such a declaration. She certainly wasn't about to tell him she was close to falling for him either. That would only give him power over her. He had enough of that already.

No, she wouldn't be foolish enough to admit that. But she would think about going to New York with him and, when he asked her again, she probably would say yes.

'That steak was quite good,' Ben said, wiping his mouth with a paper serviette.

'My dad cooks much better steak on the barbecue,' Jess told him. 'And Mum's salads are way better.'

'In that case, I'm in for a treat later today.'

'Just don't let my brothers give you too much beer.'

'Why? You're worried I might not be able to perform when you take me home?'

'What? No, of course not! Ben De Silva, haven't you had enough sex for one weekend?'

'There's no such thing as too much sex.'

'There is if it involves getting your bottom spanked,' she whispered so that the people at the next table couldn't hear.

He frowned. 'Sorry. I did get a little carried away last night. In that case, you can have today off.'

She tried to be annoyed with him but she simply couldn't. Instead, she smiled. A slightly wry smile, but still a smile. 'One day, some woman is going to tell you where to go, Ben De Silva.'

He nodded. 'You could be right there. And I have a feeling she's sitting across the table from me.'

I wish, Jess thought. But she just laughed, then finished off her coffee. Ten minutes later, they were back on the road and heading for home, turning off the motorway just after three-thirty.

CHAPTER NINETEEN

JESS'S HOME WAS bigger than Ben had expected, a two-storeyed, family-sized house in blond brick, with the biggest shed that Ben had ever seen sitting in a nearby paddock. A workshop, obviously, plus garaging for the hire cars. Two of the three massive roller doors were open and Ben could glimpse several cars within. The land around the house was bigger than he'd expected too, at least five acres. It was a lovely looking property with well-tended gardens, rolling lawns and enough trees to give privacy and shade.

Jess drove her SUV off the driveway onto a large square of gravel by the side of the house, the clock on her dash showing five to four as Ben climbed out. Jess had explained on the way that the barbecue wouldn't start till five-ish, so they had some time before her brothers and their families descended upon them.

'What a lovely place,' he said straight away.

Jess smiled. 'We like it. Mum will be in the kitchen, preparing the salads. You can meet her first. This way…'

'I presume that's the office,' he said as he walked past a converted double garage which had sliding glass doors at the front with 'Murphy's Hire Car' in big, black letters engraved on it.

'Yes,' she said. 'That's mostly Mum's domain. I help out when Mum's shopping or plays bowls or just needs a break. Mum, we're here,' Jess called out as she opened the front door.

A woman appeared at the end of the hallway, light behind her forming the silhouette of someone much shorter than Jess, and somewhat plumper.

'Goodness, but you made good time. I didn't expect you till four-thirty at least.'

When she came forward, Ben saw her more clearly. She looked nothing like Jess, being short, with ash-blonde hair and blue eyes. Attractive for her age, though.

'Hello, there,' she said, smiling as she looked him up and down. 'You must be Ben.'

'And you must be Mrs Murphy,' he replied, stepping forward to give her a kiss on the cheek. 'Lovely to meet you.'

Jess could not believe the look on her mother's face. It was the kind of look you saw on the face of a female fan of a rock star. Truly!

'Oh, don't call me that.' Her mother fairly simpered at him. 'Call me Ruth.'

Jess gained some satisfaction in the thought that he wouldn't charm her father so easily. Joe Murphy was a tough nut to crack. He wasn't going to be impressed by a New Yorker who'd never had dirt under his fingernails in his life.

'In that case, Ruth,' Ben said, flashing those brilliant white teeth of his, 'would you kindly point me to the nearest bathroom?'

Her mother didn't point. She escorted Ben herself to the small powder room next to the family room, leaving Jess standing there in the hallway like some shag on a rock.

Jess sighed, then trudged upstairs to use the toilet in the main bathroom. By the time she made it downstairs, Ben was ensconced on one of the kitchen stools, chatting away happily to her mother whilst she worked on the various salads.

'That's a terrific new name Ben's come up with for Fab Fashions, isn't it?' she directed at Jess as she joined them.

'Fantastic,' Jess agreed, at which Ben slanted her a narrow-eyed glance. Had he heard the slight sarcasm in her voice?

'You might get your job back there soon,' Ruth rattled on.

'You never know, Mum. I presume Dad's in the shed working on that blue Cadillac?'

'Yes, the seats finally came yesterday. He's been working on them all day.'

'I think I should take Ben out to meet Dad before the others get here, don't you?'

'Oh, but I just put the kettle on for a cup of tea. Ben says he likes tea more than coffee. Same as me.'

'We won't be long, Mum,' she said, then gave Ben a look which brooked no protest.

He slid off the stool and followed her back down the hallway and out of the front door.

'You *are* bossy and controlling,' he said as she marched in the direction of the shed with him in her wake.

'And you're a serial charmer,' she snapped.

He laughed. 'Better than being a serial killer.'

'I suggest you curtail that silver tongue of yours with my sisters-in-law. The Murphy men are known to be extremely jealous.'

'What about the Murphy women?' he threw at her.

'Them too. So watch yourself.'

'I like your being jealous.'

'Of course you do. It suits your male ego, which is insufferably large.'

'So will something else be if you keep that up. I get turned on by feisty women.'

She gave up at that point, throwing her hands up in the air in defeat.

She was glad that her father chose that moment to walk out of the shed, wiping his hands on a towel as he did so.

'I thought I heard someone,' he said, coming forward. 'You must be Ben,' he said, and held out his hand.

Ben shook it, thinking that this was where Jess got her striking looks. Joe Murphy was one handsome fellow, with thick black hair sprinkled liberally with grey and the deepest, darkest brown eyes, which at that moment were surveying him with considerable thoughtfulness.

'So, how did your weekend go?' he asked Ben, not Jess. 'The wedding go off okay in the end?'

'It was close to perfect,' Ben said. 'Jess here was marvellous, the way she stepped in. You heard about what happened, did you?'

'Oh yes, Ruth told me all about it. Look, I just have to finish a job here and I'll be over to clean up and get the barbecue ready. You ever cook on a barbecue, Ben?'

'Lots of times,' he said. 'I was brought up here in Australia.'

'No kidding; I didn't know that. So that's how your best friend turned out to be Australian.'

'Yep,' Ben said, sounding more Ocker by the minute. 'We went to school together in Sydney.'

'Fancy that.'

'So, what's this job you're doing, Mr Murphy? Can I help?'

'I doubt it. I'm just putting some new seats into an old Cadillac convertible I bought. The kids like to hire cars like that for their graduation night.'

'My dad collected vintage cars at one stage. Which model Cadillac is it?'

Jess could not believe it when they went off together, talking cars. Spluttering, she whirled and stormed back to the house, only just managing to have her exasperation under control by the time she reached the kitchen.

'Where's Ben?' her mother asked straight away.

'Helping Dad with the Cadillac, would you believe? I'll have tea, though, if you're making it.'

'Can you get it yourself, dear? I really need to go spruce myself up a bit. I can't wear this old thing when we have a guest like Ben.'

'He's just a man, Mum, not some movie star.'

'Well, he looks like a movie star. I know you said he was handsome, Jess, but he's beyond handsome, with that smile and those eyes. I've never met a man quite like him. I dare say you haven't either. He makes Colin look very ordinary. And I thought *he* was good-looking.'

When Jess sighed, her mother gave her a sharp look.

'Did something happen with Ben over the weekend that I should know about?'

Jess kept a straight face with difficulty. 'Like what?'

'You know what, girlie.'

'I think, Mum, that my sex life is my private business, don't you?'

Her mother looked at her for a long moment before smiling an understanding smile. 'Of course it is. You're a grown woman. But let me just say that I don't blame you, love. If I were thirty years younger I would have done exactly the same thing.'

Jess stared after her mother as she walked off. She'd been expecting the third degree, or disapproval, or something! She certainly hadn't expected her mother's reaction to Ben to be so blindly approving. Couldn't she see that her daughter's leaping into bed with such a man was fraught with danger to her happiness? She should have been warning her off him, not saying she would have done exactly the same thing!

Jess sighed. The man was a devil all right. With way too much sex appeal. And way too much charm. Even her father liked him. No doubt her whole family would fall under his spell in no time flat.

Still, if they did, she would at least be able to relax a bit and enjoy the barbecue instead of being on tenterhooks all the time. This last weekend might have been exciting but it hadn't exactly been relaxing!

CHAPTER TWENTY

BEN WAS HELPING Joe with the barbecue when Jess joined them, a huge black-and-white cat in her arms.

'You haven't been plying Ben with too much beer, have you, Dad?' Jess said in a teasing but loving voice which Ben could never imagine using with his own father. Or his mother, for that matter. He'd thought he had a good relationship with both his parents but seeing Jess interacting with her parents was a real eye-opener.

So was her interaction with the rest of her family. She was so warm with them, caring and considerate, asking after their well-being when they arrived with real interest, not just giving lip-service. He could see how much they loved her back as well. The children had flocked around her, vying for her attention. Even the damned cat loved her, yet he'd been warned by Joe not to touch Lazarus, as he was known to scratch. When he'd commented on the cat's name, he'd been told that Lazarus had been stillborn but Jess had resurrected him with the kiss of life.

Ben didn't doubt it. She was a girl of many talents, and a wealth of stubbornness. He still could not believe she'd refused to come to New York with him. But he had no intention of giving up on that score.

'The boys want Ben to go play cricket with them and the kids,' Jess said. 'I'll take over for him here,' she of-

fered before dropping the cat gently onto the paved per-
gola which stretched across the back of the Murphy
house.

'Can you play cricket?' Joe asked as Jess took the fork
Ben had been using to turn the steak and sausages. 'I
gather it's not a popular sport in America.'

Ben grinned. Could he play cricket or what? He'd been
captain of his school's A-grade cricket team. But best not
mention that. That would be bragging.

'Don't forget, Joe,' he replied, still smiling. 'I went to an
Australian school. A *boy's* boarding school, where sport
was compulsory. We played footie in winter and cricket
in summer.'

'Right. Off you go, then. Just don't go hitting the ball
into that thick bush over there. Can't count the number
we've lost in there over the years.'

Ben resolved to peg back his batting ability a bit. No
need to be a smart Alec.

Jess watched Ben stride off, a wry smile on her face.
If she knew Ben, he would be anything but an ordinary
cricket player. He wasn't ordinary at anything he did. He
was an exceptional man, with exceptional abilities and exceptional social skills.

She was still amazed at how he instinctively knew what
to talk about with every member of her family. He talked
cars with her father, sport with her brothers and the ad-
vances in technology with her very smart sisters-in-law.
He didn't mention his wealth when he was introduced,
or sit back and play the role of honoured guest. He was
happy to help with the food and very happy to drink beer.
She imagined that over in New York his social life was
very different. He'd go to fancy restaurants and fancy
parties where they'd eat caviar and drink the most expensive champagne.

Jess frowned at this last thought. She would be uncomfortable with that kind of life. It was shallow, in her opinion. And snobbish. And way out of her league. She was a simple girl at heart with simple wants, like love, marriage and a family. She wasn't cut out for the high life.

Such thoughts renewed her resolve not to go to New York with him, if and when he asked her again. Jess suspected she would not enjoy the experience. The sex part, yes. And possibly some of the sightseeing. New York was a fabulous city, she was sure. But she shrank from the idea of meeting any of Ben's American friends or ex-girlfriends; shrank from being looked down upon by the type of people he mixed with.

The barbecue finished early, as the younger children got tired and the older ones had to go to school the next day. Ben seemed reluctant to leave, however, staying to help clear up and to have a final beer with her father. It was after ten before Jess could drag him away.

'You have a wonderful family, Jess,' was the first thing he said on the way back to Blue Bay. 'You're very lucky.'

'Yes, I am,' she agreed. 'By the way, my mother knows about us.'

His head jerked her way. 'You *told* her?'

'No, she guessed. Like I said, she's very intuitive.'

'How much does she know?'

'No details. Just that we've had sex.'

'That's good, then. She won't worry if you get home late.'

'She'll still worry. That's a mother's job. Frankly, I was surprised at how calm she was over my sleeping with you.'

'That's because she knows I'm one of the good guys.'

'Hmm. I doubt that's the reason. Now, I'm not coming

inside with you tonight, Ben,' she went on firmly, determined not to weaken and be seduced by him. Again. 'I'm
dropping you off and going straight home.'

'Fair enough.'

She blinked her surprise at his easy acceptance of her
stance. Maybe he was tired. Yes, that was probably it. He'd
had a very tiring weekend.

In no time she was pulling into the kerb. She did get
out to open the boot and, yes, she let him give her a kiss
goodnight after he'd placed all his things on the pavement.
Not too long a kiss, as it turned out, both their heads lifting when his phone rang. Frowning, Ben rifled the phone
out of his pocket and stared at the ID.

'Damn,' he said. 'It's Amber.'

'Aren't you going to answer it?' Jess asked, trying not
to sound as sick as she was suddenly feeling.

'I might as well,' Ben said. 'She has to know sooner or
later that it's over between us.'

He put the phone to his ear. 'Hello, Amber. I thought
you said we weren't to contact each other till I got back.'

Jess just stood there, listening to a one-sided conversation, her stomach tight with tension.

'What?' he suddenly snapped. 'Say that again?'

Jess watched as Ben suddenly lost all his normal glow,
his face going a ghastly ashen colour. Whatever Amber
was telling him had to be dreadful.

'No, no,' he choked out. 'I'll come home straight away.
Tell the funeral home to delay things till I can be there to
make the arrangements.'

Jess's heart sank. She could think of only one person's
funeral which would make Ben look this way. His father
must have died. Oh, dear God, poor Ben…

'No, I don't want you to help,' he was saying, his voice
under control again. 'No, Amber, I don't want to marry you

either. I'm sorry but I've met someone else... Yes, an Aus-tralian girl... Yes, yes, I do,' he said and looked a startled Jess straight in the eye. 'I'll be bringing her back with me.'

Jess's mouth fell open. It was still open when Ben put his phone back in his pocket.

'Please don't say no, Jess. My father died of a massive coronary last night. I can't bury him alone,' he said brokenly.

Jess's heart turned over at the raw grief in his face. Even if she had decided not to go to New York with him if he asked again, she would say yes to this. How could she turn her back on the man she loved when he was at his most vulnerable? Because, of course she loved him. She couldn't deny it any longer. Not to herself, anyway.

'Yes, of course I'll come with you,' she said gently.

'Thank you. I don't know what I would have done if you'd said no. I need someone I care about by my side, Jess. If you're there, I'll make it through.'

Jess's breath caught at his words. 'You really care about me, Ben?'

'Yes, of course I do. You care about me too, don't you? I refuse to believe you're just with me for the sex.'

'Of course I'm not!' she blurted out, shocked that he would think such a thing.

He sighed a deep sigh. 'That's a relief. Let's go inside and start making plans.'

His mother's apartment was as she'd imagined it to be. Very spacious and modern with large windows, polished wooden floors and Italian leather furniture.

'I'll get onto the airline,' Ben said, 'whilst you ring your parents. You do have a current passport, don't you?' he added sharply.

'Yes,' she answered.

'Good. I'll make my calls from the kitchen. You stay here.'

Her mother answered on the second ring, her voice anxious.

'What is it, Jess? Have you had an accident?'

'No, Mum,' she said, then launched into an explanation of events.

'And you're going to go back to New York with him?' her mother said, sounding shocked.

'Yes, Mum.'

'When?'

'As soon as possible. Ben's on to the airline now.'

'But you hardly know the man, Jess.'

'I know him better than I ever knew Colin.'

'You love him, don't you?'

'Yes, Mum. I do.'

'Does he love you back?'

'I'm not sure.'

'You do realise that with his father dying he'll be a very rich man.'

'Yes, Mum. I'm not stupid.'

'But…'

'We'll talk more when I get home, Mum,' she said as Ben walked back into the room. 'Gotta go.'

'Well?' she asked Ben straight away.

'Our flight leaves first thing in the morning. We'll have to leave here around four to be there on time. But we can sleep on the plane. We're flying first class.'

First class, Jess thought with less enthusiasm than most girls would have had. She'd never flown first class before. But that was what Ben probably did every time.

'What clothes will I need?' she asked, trying to be practical in the face of her mounting concern.

'Something black for the funeral, I guess. It's cool in New York so make sure you have a jacket. Other than that, just trousers and tops and a dress for going out at night. I can buy you anything else you might need.'

Jess conceded that he could certainly afford to buy her anything she needed, now that he was a billionaire. But she didn't want him to do that. She didn't like him thinking he could buy her as well if he wanted to.

Just what was she supposed to be by his side? Girl-friend or mistress?

She doubted he had fiancée in mind. But who knew? Love did make one hope.

'How long will you want me to stay?' she asked, doing her best to sound nonchalant.

For ever, Ben thought. But he knew it was too soon to say that. Too soon to tell her that he loved her. He wished now he hadn't said as much to Amber. She was sure to be at the wake and she might say something.

Well, too bad if she did. It was the truth.

'As long as you like,' he answered. 'It's up to you.'

CHAPTER TWENTY-ONE

THEY BOTH MANAGED to sleep on the very long flight to New York, which was just as well, because as soon as they landed and were allowed to use their mobile phones again it was all systems go. Ben didn't stop making phone calls during the rather long, slow drive from the airport to wherever his apartment was located. Jess did send her mother a text saying they had arrived safely but her attention was more on her surrounds. She had never seen so many tall buildings, so many people or such thick traffic. Sydney was small compared to New York. She stopped herself just in time from gushing when she spotted the Empire State Building. She wasn't there as a goggle-eyed tourist but as Ben's support system during this very difficult time for him.

Jess remained discreetly silent in the taxi. Though, they weren't called taxis here, were they? They were called cabs. When they finally pulled up outside a swish looking apartment building, she did her best not to do or say anything gauche which would embarrass Ben. But she was seriously impressed, both by the uniformed porter who took care of their luggage, and the doorman who said hello to Ben in a very deferential manner. Inside, the lobby was just as impressive, with marble floors and a huge, fresh flower arrangement sitting on a circular table underneath a massive chandelier. The security guard behind the desk in the corner nodded to Ben as he steered Jess over to the bank of lifts against a side wall.

'Everything's arranged,' Ben said briskly once the lifts doors closed and they were alone. 'The funeral will be at two tomorrow afternoon with the wake afterwards at Dad's apartment. My apartment's not large enough to cater for so many people.'

Not large enough? Jess thought in amazement when she walked into his apartment. The main living room was ginormous with ten-foot ceilings and tall French doors which opened out onto a very large balcony. All the walls were white, which only added to the feeling of space. On them hung some of the loveliest paintings Jess had ever seen. She hardly knew which one to look at first. Or where to look at all. The furniture was obviously very expensive, an eclectic mix of modern and antique.

'Goodness, Ben,' she said. 'How many people are you expecting at the wake if this place isn't big enough to house them?'

'Two hundred, at least,' he replied. 'Dad had a lot of business colleagues.'

'What about friends and relatives?'

'Not too many of those. Dad was an only child and his parents are long gone. So are his aunts and uncles. He possibly has a few cousins somewhere but he never kept in touch with them.' Ben gave a crooked smile. 'There might be the odd mistress or two attending, wondering if he's left them anything. But I fear they'll be disappointed. Dad told me not long ago that he left everything to me.'

Ben watched Jess's eyes when he said this, wondering if his being a billionaire would make any difference to her. Quite frankly, he didn't care if it did. He loved her and he had every intention of marrying her. He understood now how his father had felt when he'd proposed to his mother. Love did have a blinding effect on one.

But Jess was nothing like his mother. Ben felt sure of that.

'Amber might be there,' he said, feeling that he should warn Jess in advance. 'Her father was a close business associate.'

'That's okay,' she said. Though it wasn't. Not really. Jess supposed there was a small part of her which was curious to meet this Amber. But she could have managed well without the experience.

The doorbell rang. It was the porter delivering their luggage.

'Leave it just inside,' Ben directed, getting out his wallet and handing the man a note.

'I'd forgotten you have to tip everyone here,' Jess said after the porter had left. What a different country America was from Australia.

'You'd better believe it,' Ben said. 'No tip, no service.'

She didn't much like that, but didn't say anything.

'Will you be staying with me in the master bedroom?' he asked her. 'Or do you want one of the guest rooms?'

'Where do you want me to stay?' she returned, suddenly feeling nervous. Realising that she loved him seemed temporarily to have banished any desire for the exciting love-making they'd shared. Now, she just wanted him to hold her in his arms and make love to her like they were normal people.

'With me, of course.'

'Okay. As long as you don't…you know…'

His eyes clouded over. 'You needn't worry. I'm not in the mood for fun and games at the moment, Jess.'

'No, no, of course not. I just…' She stopped, then let out a long sigh. 'I'm sorry. That was insensitive of me. Of course you don't want to do things like that at the moment. I know exactly how you must be feeling. When my grandmother died last year, it felt like someone had taken a huge jagged spoon and scraped a great big hole out of my heart. I'm sure that's how you're feeling at this moment. Maybe even worse. He was your father.'

He looked at her with such sad eyes. 'I think he knew something was wrong with him. They say sometimes people have a premonition of their death from a heart attack, even when there are no actual symptoms.'

'Yes, I've heard that's true,' Jess said.

'He rang me, you know. On the night before we drove out to Mudgee. It wasn't like him to ring unless it was to discuss business. But he just chatted away. And then, right before he hung up, he said, "give my regards to your mother". I thought that was a bit odd at the time. Now I think it was because he knew he was going to die and he wanted to put all that old bitterness behind him.'

Ben gave an unhappy sigh. 'I did send Mum a text in the taxi about Dad dying and she answered me; said how sad it was for me but not to expect her to fly over for the funeral. I knew she wouldn't come, that's why I went ahead with the arrangements for tomorrow. She believed Dad hated her. But she's wrong about that. I think he actually loved her.'

'Yes. Of course he did,' was all Jess could think of to say.

Just when Ben looked as though he was going to burst into tears, he dragged in another deep breath, then straightened his spine.

'Dad would expect me to be strong,' he said.

Jess wanted to tell him that tears didn't make a man weak but she knew it would have been a waste of time.

Her father had never cried in front of her, neither had her brothers. It was just the way lots of men were.

'I'll put these in the bedroom,' he said as he picked up their bags and headed down a hallway.

Jess followed him with a heavy heart.

The master bedroom was magnificent, of course. Lavishly furnished with a king-sized bed and everything anyone could possibly want, including a huge flat-screen TV built into the wall opposite the bed. Ben opened the door of a walk-in dressing room which proved bigger than her bedroom back home. She tried not to gape as she hung up her outfit for the funeral, but the extent of Ben's wardrobe was mind-boggling. How could one man wear so many suits?

She unpacked the rest of her things silently, thankful that she'd thought to bring her newest and best nightie. To wear something cheap in this place wouldn't seem right. It was made of white satin, adorned with white lace. The colour would even match the room, which was mainly white and grey, not a single piece of dark wood in sight.

'I dare say you'd like to freshen up after that very long flight,' Ben said. 'And no, I won't be joining you in the shower, so you don't have to worry. I also don't want to go out to dinner tonight. I'll order something in for us. Will Chinese do, or would you prefer something else?'

'No, no. I love Chinese food,' she said.

'Good. Take your time in the bathroom. Have a bath, if you'd prefer.'

Jess hated how sad he looked. She instinctively walked over and put her arms around him, hugging him tightly. 'It's going to be all right, Ben,' she said as one did when one didn't know what else to say.

He hugged her back for a long moment before extricating himself from her arms and giving the weariest sigh.

'Dear, sweet Jess,' he said and laid a gentle hand against her cheek. 'Maybe it will be all right. In time. Meanwhile, tomorrow is going to be hell.'

CHAPTER TWENTY-TWO

IT WAS WORSE than hell, Jess decided by five the following afternoon. Firstly, it had rained overnight and she'd frozen to death, both in the church and at the cemetery. She did have a jacket, one which matched her black crepe skirt, having chosen to wear the black Chanel-style suit she'd made to attend her grandmother's funeral. But even though it was lined it wasn't a warm outfit. Everyone else, she saw, was wearing overcoats. Some were wearing hats. She didn't even own a hat!

She'd warmed up a little during the drive from the lawn cemetery back into the city, though Ben hadn't said a word. Obviously, he'd been in a pretty bad place in his head after having to deliver the main eulogy, then watch his father's coffin being lowered into the ground. He'd held her hand so tightly whilst that had happened, she'd thought her fingers would break. She hadn't known what to say to make him feel any better so she'd said nothing.

But none of that compared to the hell the wake proved to be. Jess had felt intimidated from the moment she'd set foot in that mausoleum of an apartment Ben's father had owned. Maybe if she'd been able to stay by Ben's side she would have been able to cope better. But people kept taking him away from her, smarmy men in black suits with sucking-up manners and ingratiating voices. Everyone seemed to want his ear now that he was no longer the heir but the man himself. It was all quite sickening. And depressing.

Time ticked away very slowly spent with people she didn't know, making conversation with her about things she knew nothing about. When one particularly snobbish woman asked her what she did for a living, Jess rather enjoyed telling her that she was a mechanic. The expression on her snooty face was horrified. Anyone would have thought she'd said she was a garbage collector.

Finally, just after the grandfather clock in the main hallway struck five, an exasperated Jess scooped up a glass of white wine from a passing waiter and slipped out onto one of the many balconies, hopeful of finding some solitude and peace.

But she wasn't about to be so lucky. A svelte blonde who'd been at the funeral, and who'd stared daggers at Jess across the graveside, followed her out onto the balcony.

'Well, hello there,' the blonde said. 'You must be Ben's new girlfriend, the one he told me about over the phone.'

It didn't take a genius to conclude who the blonde was.

Amber wasn't beautiful, Jess decided. But she was attractive, and she shouted money with her super-sleek hairdo, her shiny complexion and her expensive-looking black sheath dress. No doubt they were real diamonds twinkling in her ears, Jess wished that she was wearing the diamond pendant Andy had given her at the wedding. But she'd left it at home in her jewellery case.

Despite knowing that her own outfit didn't look homemade it suddenly felt home-made. And dated. Which was silly.

'Hi,' Jess returned, refusing to feel intimidated any more today. 'I presume you're Amber. Ben told me all about you too.'

Amber's smile was not at all nice. 'Did he, now? I'll bet he didn't tell you what he and I used to get up to.'

Jess hated to think of Ben doing with this creature what he'd done with her. But there was no use pretending that some of it wouldn't have happened. Ben obviously had a penchant for erotic fun and games.

'I wouldn't dream of questioning Ben over what he did with his previous girlfriends,' she said coolly. 'What's past is past.'

The blonde laughed. 'In that case, you might be in for a few surprises, sweetie. But let me warn you…if you've set your cap at marrying the dear boy, then it might be wise to play a more conservative role. I tried to accommodate his kinky little demands and it didn't get me anywhere in the end. Not that I enjoyed any of it, but a girl will do just about anything, won't they, when there are billions at stake.'

'So it seems.'

Jess and Amber whirled at the sound of Ben's voice.

Amber went a guilty shade of pink whilst Jess just stared at him.

'Amazing what you learn after a relationship is over,' he said, still glaring at Amber. 'If I'd known your father was on the verge of bankruptcy, then I'd have better understood your sudden declaration of love. Not to mention your timely proposal.'

'Ben, I…I…'

'Save it, Amber,' he snapped.

'*She* doesn't love you,' Amber retaliated spitefully. 'She just wants your money, the way your mother wanted your father's money. For God's sake, just look at her. She's a nothing from down under. A nobody!'

Jess stepped forward and slapped Amber's face before she could think better of it. 'I do so love him,' she spat at the stunned blonde. 'And I am *not* a nobody!'

All of Amber's face went bright red, not just the palm print on her cheek. 'I'll sue you for assault, you bitch. And you too, you bastard—for breach of promise. I'll make you pay for wasting all that time on you.'

Ben's look in return was chillingly cold. 'Give it your best shot, sweetheart. I have billions at my disposal and you've got what? A dead-broke father and a dead-end job, working for peanuts in an art gallery.'

Amber opened her mouth to say something, then just whirled and stormed off.

Ben stared at Jess who was feeling somewhat shattered by the nasty incident.

'Did you mean it?' he asked her. 'Do you really love me?'

Tears pricked at her eyes. 'Of course I do. Why do you think I'm here?'

'Amber just said it's for the money.'

'Amber's a fool. And so are you, if you think that.'

'I don't think that. That's why I love *you*.'

Jess gaped at him then burst into tears. He gathered her close and pressed his lips into her hair. 'I love you,' he murmured. 'And I want to marry you.'

Jess wept all the harder. Because how could she marry this man and live this life with him? She would hate it. And soon she would hate him.

Finally, when the crying had stopped and she could gather enough courage, she pulled back from him and lifted still, wet eyes to his. 'I do love you, Ben,' she said shakily. 'Very much. But I can't marry you. I'm sorry. I just can't.'

CHAPTER TWENTY-THREE

'I DON'T UNDERSTAND why you won't marry me,' Ben raged when he finally got Jess back to his apartment. 'If you love me the way you say you do, then what's the problem? Hell on earth, Jess, I can give you anything you want.'

'That's the problem, Ben. I don't want what you can give me. I don't want to live this kind of life,' she said, sweeping her right arm around at his apartment. 'It's too much. We wouldn't have any real friends. Neither would our children.'

'That's ridiculous. I have real friends.'

'No, you don't. There wasn't a single person there to-night who was a real friend. The only real friend you have is Andy in Australia, and that's because you met him when you weren't so rich. Being a billionaire means you can't live an ordinary life, Ben. As your wife, I won't be able to live an ordinary life either. You'll want me to go to toffee-nosed dos and dinner parties all the time with people that I despise. You'll want me to stop making my own clothes. You'll insist I have a stylist and a designer wardrobe. Our children will have nannies and bodyguards and be sent to snobby boarding schools whilst we stay at home and *entertain*. I'm sorry, Ben, but that's not what I want for my children. That's not what I want for *me*.'

He stopped pacing around the living room and sent her a disbelieving look. 'You really mean this, don't you?'

'I do,' she said, even though her heart was breaking.

He swore, then strode over and yanked her hard against him. 'I could make you change your mind,' he ground out darkly.

'No, Ben,' she said firmly. 'You couldn't.'

'Even if I promise you the world?'

'Especially if you promise me the world.'

'Then you don't really love me,' he growled and threw her from him.

When she almost fell over he grabbed her again, but not so roughly this time, his expression both apologetic and desperate. 'I'm sorry. God, I'm sorry. I would *never* hurt you, Jess. But please, don't do this. I beg of you. Stay with me. I need you. I love you. I won't let you go!'

Jess was not at her best when cornered. 'You can't stop me, Ben.'

'Then go, damn you.' And, before she could say another word, *he* was gone, slamming the front door behind him.

She waited for hours but he didn't come back. She tried his phone but it was turned off. Clearly, he didn't want her contacting him. She couldn't rest, just paced the apartment, her mind awhirl with regrets and recriminations.

It had been cruel of her to reject Ben's proposal like that on the same day that he'd buried his father. It was no wonder he'd lost his temper with her. She'd hurt him. Terribly. At the same time, Jess could not deny that what she'd said had been true. She knew she wouldn't be happy living this kind of life. And he wouldn't be happy with her as his wife. They lived in different worlds. She had always led a simple life whereas Ben lived like *this*, she thought, her gaze once again taking in the sheer luxury of her surrounds.

In the end, Jess made an agonising decision. She packed,

then went downstairs and got the doorman to summon a cab for her.

'JFK airport,' she told the driver in a broken voice.

She cried all the way to the airport where she had to wait some time before she could get a flight out. Just before she boarded, she sent Ben an explanatory and deeply apologetic text message. She didn't want him to worry about where she was, but she also didn't want him to follow her. The plane she caught set down in San Francisco, where she changed planes for the long flight back to Sydney. When she checked her messages, there wasn't one from Ben.

Jess didn't sleep much on the plane—she was travelling economy—so by the time she reached Mascot she was very tired and seriously depressed. She caught the bus over to the long-distance car park where she'd left her four-wheel drive, then literally had to force herself to drive home. Fortunately, it wasn't peak hour in Sydney, so it only took her a couple of hours. Even so, by the time she pulled into the driveway at home, she was totally wrecked.

Her mother must have heard a vehicle pull up outside; the front door was flung open just as Jess staggered up to it.

'Jess!' she exclaimed. 'Good heavens. I didn't expect it to be you. I was just having morning tea when I heard a car. What are you doing back so soon?'

'Mum, I can't talk now. I have to go to bed.'

'Can you just give me a clue as to what's happened?' Ruth asked as she followed her weary daughter up the stairs.

Jess stopped at the top step. 'If you must know, Ben told me he loved me and wanted to marry me.'

'He did?'

'I turned him down.'

'You turned him down?' Ruth repeated, somewhat stunned.

'Mum, he's too rich. I would have been miserable.'

'It wouldn't have been an easy life,' her mother said, feeling terribly sorry for her obviously heartbroken daughter. But she was proud of her too. Jess had a very sensible head on her shoulders. There weren't many girls who could turn down a man like Ben.

'Mum, I have to go to bed,' Jess said, tears threatening once more.

'You do that, darling. I'll go tell your father that you're home.'

'What?' was Joe's first reaction. 'She turned him down, did you say?'

'Yes,' Ruth said with a sigh.

'Ben won't take that lying down,' Joe said. 'He'll come after her.'

'Do you think so, Joe?'

'You mark my words. That man's crazy about our Jess. He'll be on our doorstep in less than a week.'

But he wasn't.

A week went by. Then two weeks. Then three.

Still no contact from Ben, either by phone, email or in person.

Joe couldn't believe it. Ruth wasn't quite so surprised. Maybe it was a case of out of sight, out of mind. Men, she believed, fell out of love more quickly than women.

On the following Sunday, Ruth did suggest Jess ring *him*, but this was vehemently rejected.

'No, Mum, there's no point. He's not going to give up his lifestyle for me and I'm not going to give up mine for him. That's the bottom line. So he's being sensible, not contacting me. It would only delay the inevitable. And make it even harder for me to move on.'

'But you're not moving on,' Ruth pointed out, frustrated. 'You're not even sewing any more!'

'Give me time, Mum. It's not even been a month.'

It had been, in fact, three weeks, four days and five hours since she'd last seen Ben, Jess thought bleakly. And even longer since she'd slept in his arms. Which she had the night before the funeral. It had been quite wonderful to have Ben make love to her, face to face, then to fall asleep with her head on his chest and her arms around him. She would remember the way that had felt for ever.

That Sunday night, Jess dreamt a futile dream where she and Ben got married somewhere overlooking a beach. An Australian beach. Shelley Beach, she recognised after she woke. It was an upsetting dream because that was only what it would ever be. A stupid dream! God, was she ever going to get over that man? Maybe she should have said yes and been miserable in New York, for this was just as bad, living life without him. Maybe worse!

She had to work in the office that day. Unfortunately, it turned out not to be a busy day for Murphy's Hire Car with hardly any phone calls or bookings coming in. She had way too much time to twiddle her thumbs, drink endless cups of coffee and think depressing thoughts. By the time twelve o'clock came, Jess had had enough. She stood up from her desk, deciding that she needed distraction or she'd go stark, raving mad. She would go to the movies, find herself a silly comedy. Or an action flick. Putting on the answering machine, she made her way from the office over to the house where she found her mother in the kitchen, packing away the food shopping.

'Mum, I think I'll go to the movies this afternoon. Do you mind?'

'Not at all. I'll look after the office.'

'Thanks, Mum.'

Ruth Murphy watched her daughter walk off slowly, thinking to herself that it would take Jess a long time to get over Ben. A small, selfish part of Ruth was glad that nothing had come of their relationship. She could not bear to think of her only daughter going off and living in America. At the same time, she could not bear to see her so unhappy.

Sighing, she finished putting away the shopping, made herself a sandwich and coffee, then toddled over to the office. After checking the answering machine—there'd been no calls—she ate her lunch, then picked up the book she kept there for reading when the office was slow. But she'd only finished a few pages when the phone rang.

'Murphy's Hire Car,' she said brightly.

'Hello, Ruth.'

Ruth sat up straight once she detected the American accent.

'Is Jess there?'

'No,' she said, feeling both anxious and defensive at the same time. 'Jess isn't here at the moment. Are you calling from New York?'

'No, Ruth. I'm parked just down the road from your place.'

Oh, dear Lord, he *had* come after her, like Joe had said.

'I tried Jess's phone several times but it's turned off.'

'She's at the movies.'

'At the movies?' He sounded puzzled, as though he couldn't imagine why she would be at the movies at this time of day.

'She needed to get out of the house, Ben. She's been very down since she came back from New York.'

'Did she tell you what happened?'

'Yes, she did. We're a very close family. There are no secrets between us.'

'I love your daughter, Ruth. And I mean to marry her.'

Ruth was taken aback by the fierce determination behind his words.

'In that case, what took you so long to come after her?' she couldn't help throwing at him.

'I needed time to change my life so that she would accept my proposal.'

'What do you mean? How have you changed your life?'

'I would rather discuss that with Jess, if you don't mind. Though, there is something I'd like to ask her father first, if he's here.'

'Well, yes, he is. He's working on one of the cars.'

'I'll be there shortly.'

When Ben hung up, Ruth just sat there in a total panic. Clearly, Ben meant to ask Joe for Jess's hand in marriage. What else could it be? She should have warned Ben that he might not get so civil a reception from Joe. He was mad as a hatter with Ben. Alternatively, she could race down to the shed and warn Joe that Ben had come to win Jess over.

But she'd dithered too long, Ruth realised when she saw a white sedan speed past the office on its way to the shed.

Joe heard a car pull up outside, but he was underneath one of the limousines when the driver walked in, so all he saw was a clean pair of trainers and some bare legs under cream shorts.

'Are you there, Joe?' Ben called out.

Joe's temper had already flared by the time he slid out from under the limo and stood up to face his visitor. 'You took your bloody time, didn't you?' he snarled. 'My girl's been in a right state over you.'

'I'm sorry about that, Joe. To be honest, I was in a right state myself when she turned me down. Took me a day or two to see sense after she left, but then I got to thinking more rationally and I realised she was right. We wouldn't have been happy living in New York. But it took some time to fix things so that we would be happy.'

'What kind of things?'

'I would prefer to discuss that with Jess first. Let me just say that I think she'll accept my proposal after I tell her what I've done. But I guess there's no harm in you knowing that I've come home to Australia to live. Permanently.'

Joe was both stunned and relieved. 'That's good news, Ben. Really good news. Ruth will be especially thrilled. So you're going to ask my girl to marry you again, is that it?'

'That's the plan. But I want to do it right, Joe, so I'm asking you first for your daughter's hand in marriage. I know that your approval would mean a lot to her.'

Joe could not have been more pleased. Or more proud.

'You have my full approval, Ben. But I sure hope you haven't bought the ring yet.'

Ben's heart plummeted at this statement. 'You think she might still say no?'

'Hell, no. But she'll want to pick the thing herself, if I know my Jess. That's one strong-minded girl.'

'Tell me about it.' Ben laughed. 'Now, I'd better get going.'

'Good luck,' Joe shouted as Ben made his way back to the car. 'You're going to need it!' he chuckled to himself.

CHAPTER TWENTY-FOUR

NAUSEA SWIRLED IN Ben's stomach as he headed for West-field's and the movie theatre. A lack of confidence was not something he was familiar with. Admittedly, his ego had been brutally crushed by Jess's refusal to marry him back in New York. He had, in fact, lost a day or two indulging his sorry self in a serious drinking binge, which was most unlike him. But once he'd sobered up, and realised a future without Jess was unthinkable, he'd attacked all the changes necessary to his lifestyle in a very positive state of mind. Not once had he entertained the thought that he would not succeed in winning Jess over.

But now, suddenly, he wasn't so sure.

Maybe, during these last few weeks of silence, Jess had decided that she didn't love him after all. Maybe it was a case of out of sight, out of mind, rather than absence making the heart grow fonder. Her being 'in a right state', as her father had described, could have been her realising that it wasn't love she'd been suffering from but lust. Maybe she even regretted letting him do the things he'd done to her. Though, damn it, he was sure she'd enjoyed everything at the time. She wasn't like Amber, just doing what he wanted in the bedroom with an eye on his money. Hell, Jess was nothing like Amber at all. He really had to stop thinking all these negative thoughts. Negativity never achieved anything!

By the time Ben pulled into the large car park, he'd regained some of his confidence and composure. Once parked, he quickly checked Jess's mobile; it was still turned off. Climbing out from behind the steering wheel, he locked the car, then hurried into the shopping centre, heading through the food court and stopping at a spot where Jess would have to pass by as she exited the cinema complex.

Jess stood up as soon as the credits started coming up. The movie had been quite funny in parts. She'd managed to laugh once or twice. But the moment she exited the cinema her depression returned. What on earth was she going to do? Sit and have a coffee, she supposed wearily. No way was she going home yet. It was only just three.

She wandered slowly along the carpeted hallway which separated the numerous theatres, her blank eyes not registering the few people who passed her. Monday afternoon—especially on a warm spring day—was not rush hour at the movies. She did not bother to look at the advertisement posters on the walls like she usually did, not caring what blockbuster movies were about to hit the screens. Her mind was filled with nothing but one subject. She'd almost reached the food court just outside the cinema when someone called her name.

Her eyes cleared and there he was, standing right in front of her.

'Oh, my God,' was all she could say. 'Ben.'

When he smiled at her, she almost burst into tears. But she caught herself in time.

'What are you doing here?' she said, her sharp tone a cover for her confusion. She wanted to believe that he'd come for her, but it seemed too good to be true. And yet here he was, looking as handsome as ever.

'Your mother said you were at the movies. So I came and waited for you to come out.'

'You rang my *mother*?'

'I tried your mobile first, but it was turned off, so I rang Murphy's Hire Car and your mum answered.'

'Oh...'

'Is that all you've got to say?'

'Yes. No. What do you expect me to say? I'm in shock. I mean, you haven't rung or texted me at all. I thought you were finished with me.'

'It was you who finished with me, Jess.'

Her grimace carried true pain. 'I did what I thought was right. For both of us. So why *have* you come, Ben? Please don't ask me to go back to New York with you and marry you. That would just be cruel. I gave you my reasons for saying no and they haven't changed.'

'But you're wrong there, Jess. Lots of things have changed.'

'Not really. You're probably richer than ever now.' Hadn't she read somewhere that billionaires earned thousands of dollars a day from their many and varied investments? Or was it thousands every minute?

'What say we go have a coffee somewhere a little more private and I'll explain further?'

'There is nowhere here more private,' Jess said, waving at the open-plan and rather busy food court. People might not be flocking to the movies on a Monday but, since October had tipped into November, Christmas shopping had begun.

'I seem to recall there was a small coffee shop down that way on the right,' Ben said. 'Come on, let's go there.'

Jess didn't say a word as he led her away. She was still trying to work out what could possibly have changed.

The café he was referring to was half-empty with tables and booths to choose from. Ben steered her to the furthest booth where a sign on the back wall said you had to order at the counter.

'Would you like something to eat with your coffee?' he asked.

'No thanks.'

'Fine. What would you like? Flat white? Latte? A cappuccino?'

'A flat white,' she answered. 'No sugar.'

'Right.'

Jess tried not to ogle him as he got their coffee, but he looked utterly gorgeous in cream cargo shorts and a black polo shirt. His hair had grown a bit, she noted. It suited him longer. But then, he'd look good no matter what he wore or how long he grew his hair. Fate was very cruel to have her fall in love with a man with so many temptations.

As Jess waited for him to come back with the coffee, she tried to get her head around him suddenly showing up like this. Obviously he thought he *could* get her to change her mind. And maybe he was right. She'd been so miserable. And she'd missed him so much. Missed his love-making as well. Seeing him again reminded her of what an exciting lover he was. Exciting and dangerous and downright irresistible!

In the end, she looked down at where her hands were twisting nervously in her lap, not glancing up till he put her coffee in front of her, then sat down with his.

'Thank you,' she said politely, not really wanting coffee at all. Her stomach was in a mess. But she picked it up and had a small sip before putting it back down again. 'Now, would you mind telling me what's going on?'

He looked deep into her eyes. 'What's going on is that I still love you, Jess. And, yes, I still want to marry you.'

Oh, God, he *was* cruel.

'I don't doubt that, Ben, since you're here,' she replied. 'But sometimes love isn't enough.'

He reached over and touched her on the hand. 'You might change your mind on that when you hear what my love for you has achieved.'

It was hard for Jess to think straight when he was touching her. 'What are you talking about?'

'Well, first of all, I've come home to Australia to live.'

Her heart leapt. 'You *have*?'

'Yep. I knew you would never live with me in New York so I quit my job, then sold my majority interest in Dad's company to his partners.'

Jess just stared at him.

'After that, I used the money from the sale to set up a charity trust fund that gives financial assistance to people affected by natural disasters. We do seem to have a lot of them nowadays. Dad always gave lots of money to whatever disaster relief effort was going on, but he often worried if the money actually made it to where it was meant to go. I took this on board, so I'm the CEO of the fund. *I* decide when and where the money goes. The capital is safely invested so it should last for yonks. I don't take a salary or expenses myself, but I had to employ a couple of professional charity workers to oversee the day-to-day transactions and they do get paid. Other than that, all the money earned by the trust will go where it should go.'

Jess could only shake her head at him. 'You gave *all* your money away to charity?'

'Not all of it. Just what I inherited from the sale of Dad's company. Which, admittedly, was the majority of his estate. I still have his cash account—which was considerable—plus the money from the sale of his real-estate assets. When they're finally sold, that is. This includes his furnished apartment in New York and another one in Paris. They should bring in about twenty to thirty million each. If you include all the artwork he invested in over the years, you can add several more million. Though, I might donate them to various museums around the world. Yeah, I think I'll do that. The upshot is I'm still a multi-millionaire, Jess. Just not a billionaire. I knew you wouldn't marry a billionaire, but there's nothing attractive about poverty either.'

Jess's shock was beginning to change to wonder. 'You did all that for me?'

'The strange thing is, Jess, even though I initially gave away most of my money to win you back, after I actually did it, it felt good. Very good. They say there's more pleasure in giving than receiving and they're darned right. Anyway, as you can imagine, all that organising takes some considerable time, even when you're doing your own legal work. Which is why it took me this long to get here. I still might have to fly back occasionally, to attend to fund business, but Australia will be my permanent home from now on. It has to be, since I'm going to have an Australian wife. One whom I can't bear to live without.'

'Oh, Ben,' she said, the tears coming now. 'I can hardly believe it.'

Ben was struggling now to retain his own composure. 'Then your answer is yes this time?'

'Yes,' she choked out as she dashed away her tears. 'Of course it's yes.'

'Thank God,' he said, slumping back against the seat. 'I was worried you might still say no. And so was my mother.'

Jess blinked in surprise. 'You told your mother about us?'

'But of course. She's been at me to get married and have children for years. She'll be over the moon when I tell her.'

'You want children as well?' Jess said, still in a state of shock.

'Hell, yes. As many as you want. And if I know you, Jess, that will be more than one or two.'

'Yes, I'd like a big family,' she confessed. 'So when did you tell your mother about us?'

'Last night. I stayed at her apartment in Bondi. I flew in late, you see, too late to come up here. Though in the end, I stayed up even later, telling Mum everything. Then, would you believe it, I slept in. Didn't make it up to the coast till after lunch. Like I already told you, when you didn't answer your phone I rang Murphy's Hire Car and your mum answered.'

Jess was still a bit dumbstruck by everything Ben had done for her. 'I hope Mum was nice to you.'

'Very nice. So was your dad, after I asked him for your hand in marriage.'

'You actually asked Dad for my hand in marriage?'

'I wanted to do everything right, Jess. I didn't want anything to go wrong this time.'

'Oh, Ben, you make me feel awful.'

He frowned. 'Why awful?'

'Because you've done everything for me and I've done nothing for you.'

Done nothing? Ben looked at this wonderful girl whom he loved and he thought of all the things she'd done. Firstly and most importantly, she'd loved him back, not for his money but for himself—Ben the man, not the heir to billions. She'd also made him see what was important in life. Not fame and fortune but family and community. Not a high-flying social life but a simpler life, full of fun and friends and children. Oh yes, he couldn't *wait* to have children with Jess. What a lucky man he'd been the day he'd rung Murphy's Hire Car and met her.

But Ben knew if he said all that she'd be embarrassed. So he just smiled and said, 'Happiness is not nothing, Jess. You make me happy, my darling.'

'Oh,' she said, and looked like she was going to cry again.

'No more tears, Jess. You can cry on our wedding day, if you like, but not today. Today is for rejoicing. Now, drink up your coffee and we'll go buy you an engagement ring. There must be a decent jewellery store here somewhere.'

Half an hour later, the third finger of Jess's left hand was sporting a diamond solitaire engagement ring set in white gold, not as large and expensive as one Ben would have chosen.

'It's not how much it costs, Ben,' she'd told him firmly when she'd made her choice. 'But the sentiment behind it. Besides, I wouldn't like to make my very nice sisters-in law envious. They don't have engagement rings with diamonds the size of Ayer's Rock.'

Ben lifted his eyes to the ceiling. 'Fine. But don't go thinking I intend to buy a house with any constraints on it. I aim to have everything you and I want in it.'

'Fair enough,' Jess said, thinking to herself that that was fine by her. She wasn't a jewellery person but she'd always wanted a truly great house.

'Okay,' Ben said. 'Now that the ring business is all sorted out, take me along to that Fab Fashions store you used to work in.'

'But why?' she asked, puzzled. 'You don't own it any more.'

'Ah, but you're wrong there. When I sold Dad's company, that's the one asset I arranged to keep—the Fab Fashions chain. Dad's partners were only too happy to let me have it for nothing. They all consider it a right lemon, but I reckon that with your advice we could make a go of it. So what do you think, Jess? Can you help me out here?'

Jess's heart swelled with happiness. What an incredibly thoughtful man Ben was! And very clever. He knew exactly the way to her heart. And she told him so.

He grinned. 'Andy always said that no one should get between me and the goal post.'

She smiled. It wasn't every day that a girl liked being called a goal post.

'Does Andy know about your dad dying?' she asked on a more serious note.

'Not yet. They're still on their honeymoon. But they get back next week. Perhaps we could drive up and visit them one weekend soon, now that we're engaged. Stay in that nice little cottage for a night or two before they knock it down. Andy's planning on building a family home on that site in the New Year. Till then, they're living in the main house.'

Jess's heartbeat had quickened at the mention of the cottage, which immediately evoked the most wickedly exciting memories.

'That would be nice,' she said rather blandly. Wow, what an understatement! She could hardly wait.

He gave her a narrow-eyed look. Then he laughed. 'You don't fool me, Jess Murphy. You liked those fun and games as much as I did.'

'Yes,' she admitted. 'But I think they should be kept for special occasions, not an every-day event. I like the way you made love to me that night in New York, Ben. I thought you liked it too.'

'I did. Very much so. Okay, we'll keep the fun and games for special occasions, and weekends in nicely private cottages. Now, take me to Fab Fashions.'

* * *

Helen was surprised when Jess walked in on the arm of the most handsome man she'd ever seen. He reminded her of a young Brad Pitt.

'Hello, Helen,' Jess said, looking oddly sheepish. 'This is Benjamin De Silva, the American businessman who took over Fab Fashions.'

'Please call me Ben,' the American said and extended his hand. 'Jess has been telling me about the difficulties you've encountered since my order came through for you to make a profit before Christmas or be closed.'

Helen shook his hand whilst wondering what on earth was going on here.

'I just wanted to personally deliver a new order to you. There will be no closing down, and come the New Year there will be huge changes to Fab Fashions. A new name and brand-new stock, plus an extensive advertising campaign to go with it. Till then, I'd like you to put all of your current stock on sale at fifty-percent off. Get rid of it all. Oh, and one more thing—Jess has just agreed to become my wife.'

Jess was still smiling when Ben steered her out of the shopping centre ten minutes later.

'Did you see the look on Helen's face when you said we were engaged?' she said.

'She did seem a little shocked.'

'Shocked? She couldn't speak for a full minute and that's not like Helen at all.'

'Well, she soon made up for it. What do you think of her idea of stocking more accessories for the clothes?'

'It's a good one. Ladies love accessories. We already had a few bits of jewellery, but that could be increased, and I think some scarves, handbags and even shoes could do well.'

'We'll have to invite her to the wedding,' Ben said. 'She's nice.'

'She is. And so is her husband.'

'Then we'll invite them both.'

Jess's heart swelled with pride at the man by her side. He'd changed in so many ways. Still a 'take charge' kind of man, but she liked that about him. Still charming too. But there was more sincerity behind his charm. More depth of feeling.

'So, where have you parked your car?' she asked once they were out on the pavement. 'You do have a car this time, don't you?'

'Yes, I rented one till I knew whether I was going to actually buy a car or a plot in Wamberal Cemetery in anticipation of my throwing myself off a cliff after you turned me down again.'

Jess sucked in sharply. 'You wouldn't have done that, would you, Ben?'

'Nah. I would have gone back to New York, become a movie producer and made millions.'

'You're not going to become a movie producer here, are you?' Jess said, horrified at the thought.

'Are you kidding me? I'm going to buy myself a place on the beach, have half a dozen kids and take up golf.'

'You're not going to work?'

'Well, I do have Fab Fashions to sort out. I also might go into business with your dad, doing up vintage cars. I was very impressed with what he's done with that Cadillac. I could be the money man and he could do the actual work.'

'Sounds good to me, provided you've got enough money left to support me and all those children.'

'I have more than enough. Now, whilst we're making serious plans here, when can we actually get married? I'd like to do it asap.'

'Ben De Silva, I'm going to have a proper wedding. And I aim to plan it all myself. That takes time.'

'How much time? It only takes a month to get a licence.'

'It'll be Christmas in just over a month, which is a big celebration in our family. No way can our wedding be organised before then.'

'What about January? Or February?'

'I don't like January or February for weddings either. It's way too hot. How about March?'

'I can live with March,' Ben said. 'Just.'

'March it is, then,' Jess said happily. 'Now, let's go and tell Mum and Dad the good news.'

EPILOGUE

March, four months later...

THE LIGHTNING AND thunder started around ten in the morning. Jess and her parents rushed out onto the back veranda and stared up at the suddenly leaden sky, which had a rather ominous green colour.

'Murphy's Law,' Joe grumbled. 'You'd think it would leave me alone on my only daughter's wedding day.'

'It's not Murphy's Law, Dad,' Jess said, despite feeling disappointed. They'd been going to have the wedding ceremony at a picturesque open-air spot overlooking Toowoon Bay. 'It's just a storm.'

'No, it's bloody Murphy's Law!' he growled.

'I'm not going to let a little bit of rain spoil my big day, Dad. We have Plan B, don't we, Mum? We decided when we booked the Shelley Beach golf club for the reception that if it rained we could always have the ceremony there. They have some lovely balconies with nice views of the ocean and the golf course. If needs be, I'll give the club a call later. Everything will work out, Dad.'

It was at that point that it started to hail, denting even Jess's positive spirit.

'The wedding's not till three,' Ruth pointed out. 'It will probably have passed over by then.'

The hail was gone quite quickly but heavy rain continued all morning, resulting in several panicky phone calls
from Jess's bridesmaids, who were all at the hairdresser's.
None of them had stayed at Jess's place overnight, but were
due out there as soon as they'd had their hair and make-
up done. Jess reassured them that they had a Plan B, and
told them to stop worrying, after which she went upstairs
to do her own hair and make-up.

Just after midday, the rain finally stopped. The girls
arrived around one, looking gorgeous, the sun making its
appearance shortly before the bride and her four bridesmaids were due to leave.

Jess beamed her happiness at Catherine, whom she'd
asked to be her matron of honour. They'd become good
friends over the last few months. Andy, of course, was
Ben's best man. Catherine was pregnant, but only two
months gone, so hopefully there would be no last-minute
dramas. Jess's three sisters-in-law were her other bridesmaids, thankfully none of them pregnant at the moment.
Pete's wife, Michelle, had given birth to a baby girl two
months earlier but had got her figure back very quickly.
Jess had made the dresses for the wedding party, all of
them strapless and full-length. Jess's bridal gown was in
ivory silk and the bridesmaids' in a pale-yellow shantung.

The bride's bouquet, made from yellow and white roses,
reached from her waist to just above the hem of her dress.
The other bouquets were smaller with just white roses.
Jess had chosen a white rose for Ben's lapel and yellow
ones for the other men.

Ruth hadn't let Jess make *her* dress, however, choosing
a lovely blue mother-of-the bride outfit from Real Women,
which now had an excellent range of elegant clothes for the
more mature lady. After an Australia-wide marketing cam-

paign during January, the chain of stores was beginning to do quite well. No great profit as yet, but it was early days.

'See, Joe?' Ruth said a little smugly. 'I knew the sun would shine on our daughter's wedding. She's a lucky girl. Now, I must get going. See you all soon at Toowoon Bay.'

Jess watched her mother drive off in the family sedan whilst her father escorted her over to the first of the gleaming·white wedding cars.

'Your mother's right,' he said to Jess once they were settled in the roomy back seat. 'You *are* a lucky girl to snare yourself a man like Ben. But then, he's a lucky guy to have a girl as special as you for his wife. Not to mention so exquisitely beautiful.'

'Please don't say things like that to me, Dad,' Jess said, her eyes pooling with moisture. 'I don't want to cry and ruin my make-up.'

'You won't cry, darling daughter. You're too sensible for that.'

But he was wrong. Jess almost cried as soon as she saw Ben standing there waiting for her with a look of such wonder and love in his eyes. She came even closer to weeping when he promised to love her till his dying days. She definitely would have cried when the celebrant announced that they were husband and wife, but Ben saved the day by kissing her with such passion that she forgot all about tears.

After that she didn't think about crying, being swept along with all the things which had to be done—first the photos at Toowoon Bay, then more at the golf club, followed by the greeting of the guests, pre-dinner champagne on the balconies and then the official part of the reception.

She smiled her way through all the speeches. Andy was suitably funny and Ben wonderfully complimentary about his beautiful bride. She smiled during the cake-cutting and the bridal waltz. She smiled and laughed with

Catherine whilst she changed into her going-away outfit, a chic white linen dress with red accessories. She and Ben planned to spend their wedding night at the Crown Plaza at Terrigal and the following day they were setting off on that long-awaited road trip around Australia; Jess's trusty four-wheel drive was already parked at the hotel. Not only was it parked but packed with every provision they could possibly need.

It wasn't till Jess was saying her goodbyes to her parents that tears suddenly flooded her eyes.

'Come now, Jess,' Joe said in a choked up voice as he hugged her. 'You don't want to spoil your make-up, do you?'

Jess laughed, then wiped away her tears. 'Absolutely not,' she said. 'But they aren't unhappy tears. I was just thinking what wonderful parents you and Mum are.'

'Oh, go on with you,' Joe said, though he seemed pleased. Ruth, however, started to look a bit weepy.

'Jess is right,' Ben said, stepping forward from where he'd been saying goodbye to his own mother. 'You are both wonderful. So we got our heads together and decided to give you both a little personal something. Here...' And he handed Joe a rather large envelope which had a well-known travel agency's logo on the outside.

'What on earth have you done?' Joe said as he opened the envelope and pulled out the printed itinerary of a very extensive trip around Europe.

'Now, we don't want to hear any objections,' Ben went on as a very wide-eyed Ruth looked over her husband's shoulder and read where they would be going. Knowing that they weren't seasoned travellers, Ben and his mother had booked guided tours as well as a long cruise down the Rhine. It would take them a good four months to do it all, the various tours taking in almost every country in Europe, finishing in Italy.

'Your departure date is not till late April. It's not a good idea to holiday in Europe in the dead of winter if you don't have to,' he added. 'As for Murphy's Hire Car...Jess's brothers will look after that till you get back. They assured me it's not a busy time of the year, anyway.'

'But it says we'll be travelling first class,' Ruth said, amazed.

Ben's mother, who'd been standing nearby, suddenly came forward, her arm linked with Lionel's. 'Please don't worry about the cost,' Ava said. 'I have more money than I need. Besides,' she added, smiling coyly at her partner, 'Lionel has decided to make an honest woman out of me and he has buckets of money himself, haven't you, darling?'

Darling Lionel just smiled.

'Now,' Ava raced on, 'I've been to all those places in Europe and it would be a real shame for you not to go whilst you're young enough to enjoy it. Oh, and Ruth, you and I are going clothes shopping in Sydney before you leave. I know exactly what you'll need.'

Ruth beamed at her. 'I'd love that, Ava.'

'And Lionel can take Joe clothes shopping at the same time,' Ben suggested.

'I'd be only too happy to,' Lionel agreed. 'If Joe wants me to, that is.'

Joe grinned. 'Sounds good to me. Can't have Mother showing me up, can I?'

'That's all settled, then,' Ben said, looking pleased with himself. 'Then, when we both get back from our holidays, Joe, we'll get right to work on that vintage car idea I told you about.'

'Too right,' Joe said, clapping Ben on the back.

'Hey!' Jess exclaimed, pretending to be piqued. 'Where does that leave me?'

'You can stay at home and clean that big house I bought you,' Ben said.

'But I didn't want such a big house. That was your idea.'

'You didn't say no.'

The three parents rolled their eyes at each other.

'Are these two having their first marital spat?' Andy said on joining them.

'I hope not,' Joe said.

Jess and Ben looked at each other, then laughed. 'We're just kidding. We both love our house.' It wasn't on a beach; Ben had decided he needed more room if and when he had sons. Their new purchase sat on a five-acre lot at Matcham, a rather exclusive rural enclave not far from the coast. The house was huge with six bedrooms, three bathrooms, a four-car garage, a tennis court and, of course, a solar-heated pool. They had already planned to have Christmas there the following year, Jess aiming to make it a very special occasion.

Thinking this last thought sent another thought into Jess's mind.

'Is a wedding night a special occasion?' she whispered to Ben once they'd said their final goodbyes and climbed into the back of the waiting limousine.

His eyes widened in mock horror. 'Are you suggesting what I think you're suggesting?'

'Not quite. I don't want to have to drive all that way tomorrow with an iffy bottom.'

'Hush up, wife. The driver might hear.'

'You're no fun any more,' she said sulkily.

Ben had actually refused to make love to her all week, saying she had to learn to wait.

'No fun!' Ben exclaimed. 'Might I remind you what we got up to just last month in Andy's cottage?'

'Hush up, husband. The driver might hear.'

Ten minutes later, they were safely alone in the bridal suite, which was beautifully furnished and quite seductive, with its big bed and mounds of pillows.

'If you must know,' Ben said as he busied himself with the waiting champagne bottle, 'I packed a little box of surprises which might come in handy during our rather elongated honeymoon.'

Jess's heart leapt. 'What kind of surprises?'

'Just a few naughty little items which I found on a website. You'll find out if and when required. But we certainly don't need anything like that tonight. Tonight is meant for more romantic sex. Though even romantic sex requires that clothes be removed. Why don't you get naked, my lovely wife, whilst I pour us some of this splendid champagne?'

'Aren't you going to get naked too?' a fiercely turned-on Jess asked after she'd complied.

He walked over to her slowly and handed her a glass. 'All in good time, my darling,' he murmured with wicked lights dancing in his beautiful blue eyes. 'All in good time.'

* * * * *

Mills & Boon® Hardback

December 2014

ROMANCE

Taken Over by the Billionaire	Miranda Lee
Christmas in Da Conti's Bed	Sharon Kendrick
His for Revenge	Caitlin Crews
A Rule Worth Breaking	Maggie Cox
What The Greek Wants Most	Maya Blake
The Magnate's Manifesto	Jennifer Hayward
To Claim His Heir by Christmas	Victoria Parker
Heiress's Defiance	Lynn Raye Harris
Nine Month Countdown	Leah Ashton
Bridesmaid with Attitude	Christy McKellen
An Offer She Can't Refuse	Shoma Narayanan
Breaking the Boss's Rules	Nina Milne
Snowbound Surprise for the Billionaire	Michelle Douglas
Christmas Where They Belong	Marion Lennox
Meet Me Under the Mistletoe	Cara Colter
A Diamond in Her Stocking	Kandy Shepherd
Falling for Dr December	Susanne Hampton
Snowbound with the Surgeon	Annie Claydon

MEDICAL

Midwife's Christmas Proposal	Fiona McArthur
Midwife's Mistletoe Baby	Fiona McArthur
A Baby on Her Christmas List	Louisa George
A Family This Christmas	Sue MacKay

Mills & Boon® Large Print

December 2014

ROMANCE

Zarif's Convenient Queen	Lynne Graham
Uncovering Her Nine Month Secret	Jennie Lucas
His Forbidden Diamond	Susan Stephens
Undone by the Sultan's Touch	Caitlin Crews
The Argentinian's Demand	Cathy Williams
Taming the Notorious Sicilian	Michelle Smart
The Ultimate Seduction	Dani Collins
The Rebel and the Heiress	Michelle Douglas
Not Just a Convenient Marriage	Lucy Gordon
A Groom Worth Waiting For	Sophie Pembroke
Crown Prince, Pregnant Bride	Kate Hardy

HISTORICAL

Beguiled by Her Betrayer	Louise Allen
The Rake's Ruined Lady	Mary Brendan
The Viscount's Frozen Heart	Elizabeth Beacon
Mary and the Marquis	Janice Preston
Templar Knight, Forbidden Bride	Lynna Banning

MEDICAL

200 Harley Street: The Soldier Prince	Kate Hardy
200 Harley Street: The Enigmatic Surgeon	Annie Claydon
A Father for Her Baby	Sue MacKay
The Midwife's Son	Sue MacKay
Back in Her Husband's Arms	Susanne Hampton
Wedding at Sunday Creek	Leah Martyn

Mills & Boon® Hardback
January 2015

ROMANCE

The Secret His Mistress Carried	Lynne Graham
Nine Months to Redeem Him	Jennie Lucas
Fonseca's Fury	Abby Green
The Russian's Ultimatum	Michelle Smart
To Sin with the Tycoon	Cathy Williams
The Last Heir of Monterrato	Andie Brock
Inherited by Her Enemy	Sara Craven
Sheikh's Desert Duty	Maisey Yates
The Honeymoon Arrangement	Joss Wood
Who's Calling the Shots?	Jennifer Rae
The Scandal Behind the Wedding	Bella Frances
The Bridegroom Wishlist	Tanya Wright
Taming the French Tycoon	Rebecca Winters
His Very Convenient Bride	Sophie Pembroke
The Heir's Unexpected Return	Jackie Braun
The Prince She Never Forgot	Scarlet Wilson
A Child to Bind Them	Lucy Clark
The Baby That Changed Her Life	Louisa Heaton

MEDICAL

How to Find a Man in Five Dates	Tina Beckett
Breaking Her No-Dating Rule	Amalie Berlin
It Happened One Night Shift	Amy Andrews
Tamed by Her Army Doc's Touch	Lucy Ryder

1214GEN STD HB

ROMANCE

The Housekeeper's Awakening	Sharon Kendrick
More Precious than a Crown	Carol Marinelli
Captured by the Sheikh	Kate Hewitt
A Night in the Prince's Bed	Chantelle Shaw
Damaso Claims His Heir	Annie West
Changing Constantinou's Game	Jennifer Hayward
The Ultimate Revenge	Victoria Parker
Interview with a Tycoon	Cara Colter
Her Boss by Arrangement	Teresa Carpenter
In Her Rival's Arms	Alison Roberts
Frozen Heart, Melting Kiss	Ellie Darkins

HISTORICAL

Lord Havelock's List	Annie Burrows
The Gentleman Rogue	Margaret McPhee
Never Trust a Rebel	Sarah Mallory
Saved by the Viking Warrior	Michelle Styles
The Pirate Hunter	Laura Martin

MEDICAL

200 Harley Street: The Shameless Maverick	Louisa George
200 Harley Street: The Tortured Hero	Amy Andrews
A Home for the Hot-Shot Doc	Dianne Drake
A Doctor's Confession	Dianne Drake
The Accidental Daddy	Meredith Webber
Pregnant with the Soldier's Son	Amy Ruttan

MILLS & BOON®

Why shop at millsandboon.co.uk?

Each year, thousands of romance readers find their perfect read at millsandboon.co.uk. That's because we're passionate about bringing you the very best romantic fiction. Here are some of the advantages of shopping at www.millsandboon.co.uk:

* **Get new books first**—you'll be able to buy your favourite books one month before they hit the shops

* **Get exclusive discounts**—you'll also be able to buy our specially created monthly collections, with up to 50% off the RRP

* **Find your favourite authors**—latest news, interviews and new releases for all your favourite authors and series on our website, plus ideas for what to try next

* **Join in**—once you've bought your favourite books, don't forget to register with us to rate, review and join in the discussions

Visit **www.millsandboon.co.uk**
for all this and more today!